Dedicated to Freda Bateman, my muse

## Acknowledgements

My grateful thanks go to friends in Berwick-upon-Tweed, London, Manchester, Nottingham, Stoke-on-Trent and York. They read my manuscript (though the material was not necessarily of their choice...) and their interested criticism  encouraged me to keep writing.

The support of *Gay Authors' Workshop* members has made publication possible.

# PRISONER 537

## Thursday Morning 7th May 1970

Dee's eyes widen with alarm when she sees the image of her mother through the glass panel in the back door. A light knock and the door opens. No chance to warn her that the house is full of policemen. An apprehensive look on her mother's face – the presence of three police cars parked in front of the house has been warning enough. No time for the visitor to put down her bags and take off her coat before they hear, 'Deanna Livesey, I'm taking you into custody on suspicion that you murdered your mother-in-law, Madeleine Theresa Livesey...'

Her mother gasps indignantly. Bag and travelling case are dumped unceremoniously on the kitchen counter. She starts vigorously to undo buttons as if to tear herself out of her coat and deal with the situation.

'How ridiculous,' she gives vent at the same time, 'my daughter wouldn't commit murder!'

The detective turns his expressionless face toward her, 'Mrs?'

'Warburton,' she answers angrily.

'Mrs Warburton, I'm acting on evidence that my officers have collected here, at the scene of the crime.'

'Crime? What're you talking about? Here? There hasn't been any crime here! What evidence can you possibly have of a crime? Deanna what's going on?' She looks at the bleak face of her daughter.

'I'm not at liberty to say any more Mrs Warburton.' He turns his back to her, intent on making his arrest. 'Mrs Livesey, would you come with me please?'

But Dee, as she likes to be called, is at present a white-faced suspect trying to get to a seat. She's not in a fit state to answer ier's question or go anywhere with anyone. The peculiar ⸃n in her head forewarns that she's going to faint. She sets ᴏɴ. ᴀᴿᴅ a chair at the kitchen table but her legs won't move. They feel like elephant legs. She doesn't feel the strong arms that catch her.

She returns to her senses to find she's sitting on a chair with her head between her knees. A firm hand is holding her down. Her feet in her old Jesus sandals swim into view, planted on the terrazzo tiles of the kitchen floor. The completely inconsequential thought, that her toes look nice and clean, is wiped out of her mind by the sound of screaming. Of course – policemen, arrest! It's Maddy, Maddy her three year old daughter that's screaming. She had suggested to Maddy that she sit at the table and wait for her juice and biscuit. The shock of seeing her mother collapse in a kitchen-full of uniformed strangers has been too much for the poor child. She must get to Maddy.

'I'm okay, I'll be okay,' she says and sits up but she can't summon the strength to stand up.

'Deanna, you sit there for a minute. I'll see to Maddy.' Mrs Warburton scoops up her granddaughter and takes her through to the living room. The crying stops.

Dee is washed-out, the tattered shreds of her energy wiped out by this police intrusion and accusation. How can it be that the view through the kitchen window is unchanged? The sun is still shining. The lilac blossom is as beautiful as ever. The sparrows are cleaning up the crumbs on the bird table. This morning started so hopefully, with the comforting knowledge that her mum was coming to help her get over the trauma of the last few days. No trace of that hopefulness is left.

She turns as the hall door opens and Mrs Cairns, her cleaning lady, edges nervously into the kitchen. The poor woman stands awkwardly, her hands fidgeting in her overall pockets, wondering what to make of the situation. She looks small and incongruous by the side of the tall policemen. Here she is in response to Dee's invitation. "Mum will be here in a few minutes. Come down for coffee and a chat," Dee had called up to her, but the coffee's not made. The kettle's boiling on the Rayburn. The mugs are on the counter. Dee can see her kind cleaner wondering if she should do the honours. Dee shakes her head in her direction. 'Leave it for now,' she mouths.

Dee was annoyed when the stern detective and his police officers arrived half an hour ago, demanding to see her mother-in-law's bed-sit. She assumed it must be police procedure when a person died after an attempted suicide. Not feeling very gracious, she showed them upstairs as far as the landing. "You've finished in Grandma Livesey's room haven't you?" she'd called to Mrs Cairns and hearing an affirmative from Maddy's bedroom, had pointed out the door of Grandma Livesey's bed-sit. Dee had no wish to enter that room any more often than was necessary. "Let yourself out of the front door when you've finished," she said to the policemen. She did get a shock when she looked out of the landing window and saw the line of three black saloon police cars. And now, has she really to go with these officers, walk out of her home because of some idiot suspicion? The helpless, "I don't know what to do" panic subsides a little and she begins to think more clearly.

'Mrs Cairns, can you pass me the notebook and pencil that's on top of the fridge please. I must leave a note for Thea – my seven year old daughter,' she explains to the detective.

Poor Thea, – what can she write to Thea that will help her when she arrives home from school this afternoon to find that her mother has gone? It's so soon after her road accident. The child will have to suffer further upheaval in the home. How will the disappearance of her mother, added to the death of her grandma, affect the wellbeing of a seven year old child?

*My darling Thea, I have to go with some policemen who want to talk to me about Grandma Livesey's death. I hope I will be home soon.*

*If I'm not back by Saturday, Jill's party starts at two o'clock on Saturday afternoon. Daddy will take you across the road. The present for Jill is on the bottom shelf of the wall cupboard in the living room.*

*Lots of love from Mummy X X X X X X X*

'You'll let my husband know I've been arrested?'
'He's a teacher at the College isn't he?'

'Yes.'

A police officer exits by the back door to relay the information. Thea will be all right with Jon, Dee tells herself. Thea and her father established a good relationship in her early years – before Jon's infidelities started to keep him away from home. If it takes a day or two for this mistake to be sorted out, Jon can make use of his new lover, Sarah. By all accounts she's a nice woman and Thea might need a woman's care. Not so Maddy, – that won't do for Maddy. Jon has had very little time for his younger daughter, walked past her pram, rarely baby-sat and never attempted to get to know her.

'Mum!' Her mother comes through, carrying Maddy. 'There doesn't seem to be any point in you staying here. I think it would be best for you go back home.' Her voice falters. 'Will you take Maddy with you please, until everything's settled? I'm sorry.' She can't hold back the tears. 'Mum, I'm so sorry.' Grief from the whole damn mess overwhelms her. Her mum deposits Maddy on her knee and the distracted mother and child hug tightly. Maddy's cuddles are one of the great comforts in Dee's life. God! Why ever did she agree to call this affectionate little bundle Madeleine, after a mother-in-law that could do this to her? She struggles to control her sobs and says, 'Mummy has to go with the policemen Maddy.'

'Don't worry about us,' her mother says tersely, making her obvious disgust at the whole situation clear to the policemen. 'I'll pack some clothes for Maddy and we'll get the next bus. Come upstairs and help me to pack your suitcase,' she says to Maddy. 'We'll put your doll and a story book in your pink rucksack.' The novelty appeals to Maddy but she looks anxiously at her mum.

'It's okay Maddy, you go with Granny. Give my love to Granddad.' She daren't say "I'll see you soon." Her sobs break out as she watches her little daughter toddle after her granny.

'If it's all right with you Mrs Livesey, I'll leave now and catch the same bus as your mother,' Mrs Cairns says. 'I don't want to stay here on my own now this has happened.' Dee nods dumbly to show that she understands the difficulty of Mrs Cairns' position and indicates her wages' packet on the table.

'Mrs Livesey, will you come with me please,' the detective says for the second time.

Dee takes her woollen cardigan off the back of a chair and pushes her arms into its warmth. She feels chilled. At least the disgrace of this departure won't be seen by Maddy. She's safely out of the way and doesn't have to see her mother handcuffed and hustled into the back of one of the waiting police cars. They leave by the front door and Dee glances with embarrassment at the groups of people standing on the pavements, obviously wondering what's going on. Her neighbours will be thinking that the Livesey household is seriously dysfunctional. The last time they stood about like this was eight months ago, when they heard her scream and saw the crumpled heap of Thea beside the kerb. That was an accident. Thea ran across the road without looking both ways – so much for a six year old and the *Green Cross Code*. On that occasion she heard her neighbours murmur sympathetically until she and Thea drove off in the ambulance, with its siren wailing. That was straightforward. How will she explain this to them when she gets back?

It's uncanny for her to be sitting in a Police Station in her shabby work trousers and shirt. Thank goodness she and Maddy had a bath this morning and she put on clean undies and socks! Her plan was to change in time for her mother's arrival. And thank goodness she remembered her cardigan, – an interrogation cubicle in a police station is not a warm place in which to find oneself at eleven o'clock on a Thursday morning. She's given a mug of tea. The detective obviously believes she's guilty and questions her at intervals. If he's hoping for a confession he'll be disappointed. Dee writes a lengthy statement, telling her side of the story. She wonders if there is anything she can say that will prove her innocence.

She's invited to make the one permitted phone call. It has to be to the only solicitor she knows, Mr Curtis.

Mr Curtis – she only met him once, when she wanted to divorce Jon because of his love affair with one of the teachers at the college. Mr Curtis was a fledgling lawyer in his new office buildings, kind and compassionate toward her, his troubled young client. He wore a navy suit with white shirt and shiny grey tie. His hair was dark, nicely cut and sleeked back. Dee wanted to laugh when he approached with outstretched hand and sympathy written all over his face. Her advance phone call had explained the reason for her appointment but she wasn't feeling sorry for herself that afternoon. Her mind was intent on where to live when she and Jon separated – and other practical matters. But Mr Curtis' methods were impressive. He got the divorce papers to Jon so fast, that her startled husband decided to cool his love affair and stay married. Dee was prepared to give their marriage a second chance. Thea was conceived soon after. Not that Jon's decision disinclined him toward other female conquests, as his present association with Sarah proves.

A wave of relief sweeps over her. Her mother-in-law is dead. She doesn't have to put up with being the spurned wife any longer, doesn't have to make an effort to keep the family together. She knows a break-down of the marriage will have a disturbing effect on the girls. They've no idea that their mother is unhappy. Even so, when all this is over, she determines that she will phone Mr Curtis, arrange a second appointment and request divorce papers. She'd better keep those intentions to herself in the circumstances! The detective would make a meal of her plans for a re-arranged future. He would say it was evidence of "malice aforethought".

Will murder be in the field of Mr Curtis' expertise? Will he be as efficient? There's a brief silence at the other end of the phone after she explains her situation, then his incredulous question.

'Did you push your mother-in-law out of the window?'

'I did not!'

That seems to convince him. He offers to get a good defence lawyer. Does mention of a defence lawyer mean trouble? She's hoping to return home tonight, or in the morning.

No going home! Her spirit plummets when the cell door shuts her in with the smell of disinfectant, a thin pillow and blanket, and the gradually dawning realisation that all this is in earnest. She hasn't seen a grey-brown blanket, like the one on the bed, since she chopped one up for strips to weave into a rug at night-school classes in Oldham. The tough rug is still in use in the downstairs cloakroom. She and Jon were happy then. There was a pea-soup fog one night, despite the fact that most of the factories had closed down. The buses stopped running and she had to walk the three miles home. Jon was worried because she was so late. They laughed because she was black from head to foot. He ran a hot bath for her. They never laugh these days. Hers will not be the only tears that have soaked into the flat pillow in this holding cell.

Her thoughts are in turmoil. How have her good intentions and hard work ended so dismally? Two years! For two years she's looked after Jon's mother because she and Jon both thought it was the right thing to do. Jon's mother had her accident when she was eighty-four – fell backwards off a stool when she was hanging curtains. It didn't seem wise to let her live on her own any longer. Their house with its four bedrooms could easily accommodate Grandma Livesey.

She had no time to think the situation through, how it would affect the household or the marriage, how it would affect her. Family, – wasn't it dinned into daughters that they must do the right thing by members of the family? She did just that. Chased up to the hospital in Manchester with night-wear and toiletries and then dashed back home to assemble furniture and TV so that when Grandma Livesey recovered, and came to live with them, she would have a comfortable bed-sit.

She soon understood that Jon's decision to move his mother into their home was an opportune manoeuvre on his part. He had no time for his elderly relative. He was horribly impatient with her and yet she adored him, her handsome academic son, – born to her great surprise and pleasure when she was forty-six years old. Dee used to cringe at the way the handsome son spoke to his mother.

Dee had fallen for Jon's looks, his high brow and dark hair, his smiling blue eyes and aristocratic nose and particularly his "savoir faire" re dining out, the cinema and theatre. Her Aunty Janet said he looked like Ivor Novello but Dee thought he looked like the learned men in the portraits on the ground floor of the National Portrait Gallery. Did they feel free to marry, have a good housekeeper-wife and take mistresses?

Too late Dee realised that the addition of his mother to the household was for Jon's benefit. He was no longer inconvenienced by having to travel up to Manchester to make reluctant visits. That gave him more time to follow his pursuits. The elderly newcomer was left to Dee's willing hands and her reward?

Attempted suicide. Weariness and rage battle with each other. Eventually, weariness wins and the unhappy detainee drifts off into an uneasy sleep.

The slice of toast and marmalade and mug of tea are not easy to swallow in the morning. How to chew and swallow as normal when under suspicion for murder, when one's world is upside down? Dee only managed to sleep for short periods. She was disturbed by loud voices and yells and banging doors. Police work doesn't stop overnight. No one was concerned that a tired frantic mother was shut away from everything and everybody that constituted her life.

At ten o'clock, she's relieved to be led out, handcuffed, and taken to a specially convened court. The room is panelled with wood, dark and dismal, rows of empty brown leather seats. Jon's there. He looks tense and anxious and can't manage to smile convincingly. The two of them are not allowed an opportunity to speak. Dee doubts that innocence has any credibility in such dreary surroundings. The unpleasantly familiar arresting officer presents the evidence.

'Madeleine Theresa Livesey's death is consistent with a fall from a great height. It's obvious from the position of the fingerprints on the window frame that she tried to prevent herself from being pushed out of the open window.'

Dee doesn't have time to close her gaping mouth before her considerate little request to Mrs Cairns is brought to the attention of the court. "Can you clean Granny Livesey's room and make it look a bit different for Mum, please?" Yes, she did say that. She wouldn't like to sleep in a room whence the occupant had departed via the window in an attempt to kill herself, only two days' earlier. She hadn't wanted her mother to feel uncomfortable in Granny Livesey's bed-sit. Now, in the hands of this beastly detective, her request is twisted into evidence against her – is documented as artifice to outwit the Police!

The detective has sheaves of notes, information about herself. What a busy man he must have been, to collect so much information in only three days. The Almoner's report of her vehement behaviour at the hospital is read out.

'Mrs Kenwright, the hospital almoner, said that Mrs Livesey spoke wildly. She stressed that she was not prepared to have her mother-in-law back in the family home.'

Yes, she probably did sound wild. She was extremely upset on Wednesday morning after the traumatic event the night before. Her mother-in-law was still alive. She did not want to entertain the possibility of her children witnessing a repeat performance of the suicide attempt. But the message for the assembled court is clear and condemnatory. Mrs Livesey wanted to be rid of her mother-in-law.

The Doctor's account, dated 1969 is next, – her tired and desperate plea. The detective reads it aloud.

'Mrs Livesey said, 'Please get my mother-in-law out of the house.''

She meant into hospital! She'd nursed Grandma Livesey through the worst of pneumonia and wasn't well herself. All she needed was a few days, without the extra responsibility of a sick old woman, in which she could recover her strength. Good God! How could they misinterpret her harmless request in this way?

Grandma Livesey's death must have prompted the Health Visitor to re-consider their discussion about alternative accommodation for her mother-in-law. The Health Visitor told Dee that it was the policy to keep families together wherever possible. Dee had asked if something could be done in Grandma Livesey's case, in the light of the marriage difficulties. This morning the detective interprets that discussion as part of a strategy to disencumber herself of her mother-in-law. She agreed with the policy originally in the hope that it might save her marriage – she must have been in cloud cuckoo land!

And then the medicine, – Granny Livesey had been feeling nervously unwell and the doctor had prescribed Sodium Amytal. The remaining tablets had been counted by the police, dates and numbers calculated. The conclusion was that there were some tablets missing. Of course there were! Grandma Livesey OD'd on them when they were first prescribed. In her estimation, if she took more than the prescribed dose she would soon feel better. Her behaviour became confused as a result. Jon and Dee agreed that Dee should take over the dispensation of the tablets.

It never occurred to Dee that the tablets would be saved for an overdose. She wasn't a nurse. Should she have stood over Grandma Livesey to see that she took her tablets? Her mother-in-law was intelligent and capable and, despite her eighty-six years, Dee never doubted her faculties. Dee knew she was only tolerated by Mrs Livesey senior as a good housekeeper for her son and a capable mother for his children. She was not of the Catholic faith and was not an academic. No doubt about it – supervision of tablet-taking would not have been welcome from her daughter-in-law.

None of Dee's responses and declarations of innocence carry any weight with the court officials. She's forced to presume that the unfavourable evidence will bring in a verdict of guilty. She waits tensely for what she fears is a predictable outcome. Her dread increases as the presiding Councillor slowly turns the pages of his diary. He makes an entry and fixes his attention on Dee.

'In the light of no evidence to the contrary, and taking into account the suspicious actions of Deanna Livesey in connection with the death of Madeleine Theresa Livesey, I advise the Court that she be placed on remand at Her Majesty's Stonebridge Women's Prison for a period of three months. Bail is disallowed. The date for the next hearing of this case is fixed at, Friday 31$^{st}$ July 1970.'

# WEEK ONE

Friday 8<sup>th</sup> May

Three months! Twelve whole weeks of a remand sentence based on false supposition – a reminder (as if she needed one) that truth can't easily be justified.

Dee is furious that she wasn't allowed to talk to Jon before she was thrust into prison transport. Why the hurry? A few minutes of conversation wouldn't make her any more or less guilty. Has Jon to be kept clear of complicity? Why isn't he under suspicion? Why is it assumed that she has killed her mother-in-law? Jon was in the house on Tuesday night. He could have crept up the stairs without being heard and done the deed. But it's obvious to one and all that he had no reason to hasten the death of his mother. His life is A-okay. He barely reckoned with his mother's presence in the house. In the eyes of the court, she is the disgruntled wife, the person most likely to commit murder.

Her mind is crazy with worry as the vehicle carries her further and further from her home. Thea will already be upset and now she must manage without her mum for three months. What about her own friends, the other mums at the school gate, her pals in the dramatic society? Will they believe she's guilty? Please God they won't change their attitude to Thea, take it out on her.

Granny and Granddad will reassure Maddy, she's in familiar surroundings. But the neighbours and friends near her mum's home, how will they react? At least her family will believe in her innocence but they'll probably have to deal with awkward questions. She can't think straight, her mind is rushing about all over the place. Newspapers, – will there be a report of her condemnation in the local paper? Does this type of story get broadcast? What if they show her photo on television! Surely a mother-in-law story won't make front page news but can anything ever be the same again? Her garden, – she's just got it looking great. In three months it will be overgrown.

Dee is handcuffed to a police woman. The latter doesn't attempt to engage her in conversation which is a relief as she's too preoccupied and miserable to talk. She assumes that their destination has been reached when the vehicle halts with the motor still running and voices shout directions. Electric gates whine and the vehicle drives forward. The second time it stops, Dee and her companion are instructed to get out and walk toward Reception. The handcuffs are removed and the police officer leaves for her return journey.

Admission to prison follows. The imprisonment warrant is handed over, her fingerprints are taken, her watch, wedding ring, handbag and clothes dispatched. She has to take a shower and sits in a thin gown shivering with cold and anxiety.

There is one nice surprise.

'Some time since you've been to a hairdresser,' the Reception Officer barks at her.

Well, yes it is. She usually lines herself up with two mirrors in the bathroom and trims her own hair. The memory of her contortions with comb, scissors and mirror, as she turns her head to make sure she's got the back level, makes her smile. The smile wrinkles the creases at the corner of her deep-set hazel eyes. The officer looks at her curiously. She's probably wondering what can possibly amuse this latest arrival. The officer wears her brown hair very short, above her ears, but it's well styled and suits her strong capable face, atop her strong capable figure – a veritable gate-keeper. One wouldn't contemplate running off when she's around, though the idea of being restrained by those arms and clasped against that ample bosom would make for a nice soft cuddle. Dee's eyes laugh again. She really must take her situation more seriously.

'Marylyn, get up to Reception quick and bring your bag of tricks,' the officer shouts into the phone and to Dee she says, 'Marylyn will tidy you up before you meet the girls. Prison procedure where considered advisable, courtesy of the Governor.'

So much for Dee thinking that her hair looked okay. 'What about the cost,' she remembers to ask. 'I haven't any money.'

'Ha! Never mind about that,' the officer calls over her shoulder, 'let's say Marylyn's earning her keep.'

Marylyn arrives in a hurry and dumps her bag of tricks on the table. Her crown of peroxide waves is a good advertisement for her trade but the face beneath has a tightly drawn mouth and eyes that dart everywhere, avoiding those of her client. Dee takes note of the pale blue shirt and jeans underneath Marylyn's overall, prison uniform?

'Never a bloody minute,' her hairdresser says under her breath, while Dee's head is over the wash basin. 'Sometimes I wish I had a job in the sewing room.'

'I didn't think I'd be getting my hair done in prison.'

'It doesn't look as though you think about your hair at all, Duck.'

'Hey, it's not that bad. I chop bits off when it gets too long.'

'That's what I would have thought from the look of it. You don't do yourself any favours. Prisoners get a hairdo in here thanks to the Governor. She thinks it's good for morale. If you've got a trade and she trusts you, she encourages you to work at it while you're doing your time. Mirror please, Officer Hill.'

Dee guesses they won't have use for a schoolteacher.

The mirror is hung up and Marylyn starts cutting. 'I'm not supposed to ask you this but,' she lowers my voice, 'what are you in for?'

'Murdering my mother-in-law.'

The scissors hesitate for a second and Marylyn's eyes rest briefly on the reflection of Dee's face in the mirror. She returns to the job in hand but says, more as a statement than a question, 'You didn't did you?'

'No, I didn't.' Dee is in danger of weeping when she hears this vote of confidence. She wonders if the balance of her mind is less than steady when, in rapid succession, she can alternate between finding things funny and wanting to cry. Is she more than emotionally disturbed if kindness can move her like this? 'You're from the Potteries?' she says to bypass the wobbly moment.

'How d'you guess?'

'It's where I live and the only place where people are addressed as Duck, as far as I know.'

Marylyn face brightens with a nervous smile and she continues with her styling. Dee doesn't talk to her. Hairdressers have to listen to a lot of confidences while they work. She's not prepared to burden Marylyn with her problems and from Marylyn's expression, she's sure her hairdresser has troubles of her own.

'I can't believe how good I look!' she exclaims when Marylyn has finished. 'My hair's never been so short and neat. It suits me really well doesn't it?'

'I have to say you look better than you did a few minutes ago,' Marylyn admits, quite pleased with her success. She tumbles her tools into her bag of tricks and heaves it off the table. 'See you when you're due for a trim.'

That takes away some of the pleasure in her new hairstyle. Dee reckons it will be six weeks before she needs a trim, two trims and it will be time for her hearing. Estimated like that, a three month sentence doesn't seem long – but she hasn't got through the first day yet.

The next experience is not pleasant. The room in which she waits is painted grey-green, not cheerful or warm. The door flies open and in breezes a lady doctor, her white coat unbuttoned. The doctor leafs through the papers in her hand and reels off instructions to the accompanying nurse. Dee admires her slim figure, fine intelligent features and head topped with dark curly hair. The doctor glances in her direction, then at her watch and announces to the room in general, 'I can only spare five minutes. Papers for this one please Officer Hill.'

Dee qualifies her first favourable impression of the woman. Intelligent she might be, but she could show a little more respect for a fellow human being. Dee objects to being referred to as, "one". Her oneness is not disposed to like this doctor. The papers arrive with an apologetic, 'Sorry Doctor Tupman.'

It's a medical that Dee is not likely to forget. 'Read the letters.' 'Get on the scales.' 'Stand up tall.' 'Open your gown.' 'Do you take any medication?' 'Do you smoke?'

Dee shakes her head. She's not going to honour the doctor with speech. She could tell her that she packed in smoking last year after a second dose of bronchitis. Doctor Tupman checks her watch again.

'Okay nurse, no problems with this one. All done here Officer Hill,' she calls. 'Hope I can make it to the hospital in twenty minutes.'

Dee doesn't get another look. In the doctor's eyes she's a murderer.

'Get your clothes on,' Officer Hill says.

'My own clothes?'

'Prisoners on remand wear their own clothes.'

'But I've been wearing them since yesterday, I need clean underwear.'

'We've a stock of spares until you get your stuff sent from home.'

Dressed in a washed out pair of denim bib and brace overalls and a faded tee shirt, Dee is handed her supply of bed linen. An Officer Grundy appears to conduct her to her cell. She's quaking. Everything's happening so fast. She wants to slow it all down so she can take stock of the situation. Nothing in her life has prepared her for this. Officer Grundy escorts her along corridors, unlocking and locking gates and doors. They clang. The clang echoes. She hears strident voices shouting. She's doing her damndest to control her fear by breathing deeply. They arrive at Room 15 and go through the open door.

'This is your room,' Officer Grundy says. 'New prisoner, 537 Livesey,' she calls out to the occupants and walks away.

No one moves, or speaks. Unfriendly eyes stare at her. There's one bunk bed in the room and the top bed is made up. A woman is lying up there stretched out. She raises herself on one elbow and waves the fingers of her free hand in greeting. Her chestnut brown hair is worn in a long pigtail over her shoulder; wavy tendrils escape from the tightly drawn back locks. Her smile is bright and friendly.

'Welcome fellow crim,' she says and lies down again. The woman speaks well, an educated voice with no trace of an accent.

Dee assumes that the bottom bunk will be her bed for the next three months, but three girls are sitting on it and one is lying down behind them. They're so young, seen from her motherly thirty-two years. She puts her bundle down on the table and says 'Hi.' No answer.

'What're you in for?' The woman in the top bunk asks without moving.

Dee is cautious. Marylyn implied that this is a "no go" question in prison.

'Tell me why you're here first,' she challenges.

'Ho, ho, cheeky with it,' says the voice, not unpleasantly. 'Our stories we will unfold to you later. You're the star, assuming this is your first time inside. You're today's source of interest. Tell.'

'Yes tell, you cautious bitch,' says a mocking voice from the hidden supine form on the bottom bunk. 'Answer the woman's fucking question Livesey. How come you've been sent down?'

'I'm accused of murdering my mother-in-law.'

'Did you murder her?' The pretty blonde girl sitting on the bed asks.

'No, but obviously the authorities have come to the conclusion that I did.'

'Oh my God, another posh cow that's sure of herself,' the bottom bunk mocks. 'Are you listening up there Madam Contrary? We've been sent another toffee nosed bitch; we're going to be overrun with them. So, spill it Livesey, how are you supposed to have finished her off?'

'I'm supposed to have pushed her out of the bedroom window.'

There's silence as they digest this information.

'Did you?' The blonde girl repeats her question.

'No.'

'Another one on a bum rap,' the recumbent figure says with disgust.

'Yeh, get a load of Miss Innocence. We all try that on,' the seated, mixed race girl says belligerently.

'Was it manslaughter?' The plump auburn haired girl is intrigued.

'Murder.'

'Premeditated?' The plump girl really curious.

'Premeditated.'

'Christ!' All three girls together. The top bunk takes a second look at Dee but doesn't comment.

The murder information commands attention and gives Dee a clue. Perhaps an initial awe will act as protection until she's weighed up the situation. Can she convince them that she's capable of murder?

'How old was she?' the auburn hair.

'Eighty-six.'

'Poor sod! Couldn't you wait for her to die, you miserable twat?' the snide dark girl.

Dee doesn't answer.

There would have been a lot more questions but the cool customer on the bottom bunk extricates herself from her companions and stands up. She's good looking, older, twenty-five or six, hair worn in a long bob and two large gold hoop earrings in her ears. How does she get away with wearing earrings in prison? She has noticeable brown eyes, well emphasised by the carefully plucked arch of her eyebrows. Her mouth is perhaps too small and her rose-bud lips sneer. The confidence with which she slips her hands into her jeans' pockets and leans up against the bed-support fascinates Dee. Nor is it just her face that's worth looking at. Her pronounced cleavage, skilfully accentuated by the carefully knotted shirt is meant to attract, as is her bare waist. Dee smiles, she'd like to try tying her own shirt like that, but she can hear her mother saying, "That woman is forward. Look at the way she flaunts herself."

The atmosphere in the room is tense. The woman on the top bunk is now sitting cross legged, watching.

'Well Livesey,' the sexy woman drawls, 'welcome to our little abode. My name is Tracy Manners and with a name like that it's incumbent on me to introduce the present company.' She gestures first to the plump auburn haired girl.

'My name's Gail Thompson.'

'Bel Wrigley, how d'you fucking do,' snarls the hostile blonde girl.

'Rita Dawson,' the dark girl barely parts her lips to get the words out.

'Your turn, Contrary,' Tracy addresses the woman up aloft.

'Mary Burns at your service,' she says and smiles.

'Never mind the service bit, Contrary. Livesey's on my patch and I'll be doing the servicing.'

There's a whoop of laughter from the three girls. Mary Burns shrugs as though she doesn't care.

'To continue,' Tracy says, 'you and I will share this luxurious accommodation, Livesey, and as your eyes don't miss much, I've been watching you smile, we'll be the closest of fucking companions.' She drops her voice to a seductive low. 'I mean literally of course.'

That startles Dee.

'Don't go on at her,' Mary protests. 'Leave her alone and let her settle in.'

'How long are you in for?' Tracy takes no notice.

'The Hearing is scheduled for three months from now.'

'Listen to that bit of information girls. Three fucking months! We've hardly time to welcome her and she'll be gone.'

She saunters behind Dee, slips her hands under her bib, cups them over her breasts and presses her against her ample frontage. Dee holds her breath. The sensation isn't painful or unpleasant but the suddenness of the advance, and from a woman, adds shock to this altogether alarming day.

'Not bad, bit fat,' Tracy states and resumes her provocative pose.

Dee sinks onto one of the wooden chairs.

'Stop it Tracy. Look what you're doing to her,' Mary objects for a second time.

'Shut it Contrary! See why we called her that Livesey? Always interfering, Mary, Mary bloody contrary, thinks she knows better than the rest of us.'

Dee looks up gratefully at the woman who is trying to make things easier for her.

'Bloody hell Tracy, do you have to feel her up while we're here?' Bel Wrigley asks peevishly.

'Bel Wrigley, you jealous never satisfied bitch,' Tracy shouts gleefully and Dee watches astonished as she flings Bel back on the bed, puts her hand inside her shirt and smothers her face with kisses. Bel struggles free. They both sit up flushed and laughing and adjust their shirts but Tracy's attention is still on Dee. She hasn't finished taunting her.

'Gail, you're on kitchen duty. In the morning, tell Cook that Livesey needs to be put on a diet, – Manners says her tits are too fat.'

The three girls snigger derisively. Dee is alerted to the fact that Tracy Manners is manipulative. She must have a position of power in the wing if others do whatever she suggests. When Dee glances at the top bunk she sees that Mary is following the conversation.

'Are you a dyke?' Gail asks suddenly.

Dee only knows that dykes are banks of earth controlling the water level in the Fens, what's this other use of the word dyke? Her bewildered expression reveals her ignorance.

'Christ Almighty! She doesn't know what a dyke is,' Bel sneers.

'What an ignorant bitch,' Rita breathes, hardly able to believe it.

'It's not the end of the world if she doesn't know the meaning of the word dyke,' Mary interrupts. 'The origin of the word's uncertain Livesey. There was a Greek goddess of moral justice called *Dike* but otherwise the term has been used for a lesbian since the forties. Bulldyke, baby dyke, femme dyke, lipstick, stealth dyke, whatever... I'm a stealth and lipstick dyke. When I get out, I'll behave in public as if I'm heterosexual. The assembled company wants to know if you're a lesbian.'

'There you go again, shooting your mouth off, Contrary,' Tracy complains. 'Stuff your superior wisdom up your arse. It didn't do you much good. You still ended up doing bird.'

Dee's mind is working overtime at the mention of lesbianism. She can't give an outright "no" to the question and she's no good at thinking up clever replies. She fell in love with three women teachers at Grammar School, one after the other. When lesbianism was mentioned as part of a dinner time conversation, at a county hockey training weekend at *Lilleshall*, she confessed that she'd often wondered about her sexuality. The coach sitting opposite her, immediately quashed the subject by saying, "You've a warm and loving nature," and she accepted the statement.

There was the time when she was mortified at her naiveté, on the school trip down the Rhine. She joined in the staff discussion about an unusual co-traveller. "He is queer isn't he?" she remarked. A horrified deputy head shushed her. Why, what had she said? "Queer is the name given to homosexuals," the physical education teacher whispered.

Then there was the incident with her friend Irene, when Jon was away on a walking holiday and Thea and Maddy were at her mother's caravan. She and Irene were both tipsy after a gloriously abandoned drinking and late-night dancing-session at the local night club. Irene went upstairs to the bathroom and descended the stairs without her dress, a vision in black lace undies, wanting to be loved. Pleasing a friend sexually didn't identify one as a lesbian did it? Help!

'Livesey can't make her mind up.' Tracy's look is searching.

'Perhaps we can help her to decide,' Bel says dryly. 'Lesson one, question one. What does a lesbian look at first in a woman? Answer, her breasts.'

It isn't the moment for Dee to say that, as far as lesson one is concerned, she's not in the beginners' class though up to now she hasn't reckoned that it's unusual to appraise women's bosoms, or has she? It has crossed her mind before today that she likes looking at women. Does that make her a lesbian? Surely not! The Irene episode was a one off. The morning after, she said to herself very definitely, "Now I know I'm not a lesbian." She hadn't felt any different. Panic! Did the fact that making love to a friend came naturally mean that she could be a lesbian, a dyke?

'We haven't got all day,' Rita snaps.

'I reckon that Livesey is ready for lesson two,' Manners says pointedly, breaking into the middle of Dee's confused thoughts.

'Don't worry,' Gail tries to reassure her. 'They're not all like us in here. There's plenty of 'hets'. It just happens that you're twinned with the best lover in the Wing.' She laughs spitefully. 'You won't miss your husband for the next three months.'

This is supposed to stop her from worrying! A bell rings.

Mary drops down from the top bunk and the five of them file out of the open door.

'Follow us if you want some food,' Gail calls over her shoulder.

A scared Dee Livesey tails behind them to the refectory.

## Friday Evening 8th May

In the refectory there's a space at the table for eight where her new acquaintances sit. She's quizzed again.

'Have you any kids?

'Two girls, seven and three.'

'Husband?'

'In name only,' she answers.

'Doing the dirty?' She nods.

'Men! They're more fucking trouble than they're worth.'

'Try a fucking woman then darling,' Tracy says lazily.

'Did The Penny interview you this afternoon,' Gail asks. Dee looks blank. 'She's the Governor – interviews new prisoners – if they're lucky. You're better off being interviewed by her than by Morgan.'

'Morgan's all right,' Tracy puts in quickly, – 'she's the Deputy Governor,' she adds for Dee's benefit.

'Well you would know.' Bel says bitchily.

'Just hope you get The Penny,' Gail says trying to be kind. 'The Penny's gorgeous, wait till you see her.' There's a chorus of agreement, expressed in lascivious laughs. 'We'd all like to get her into bed,' Gail enthuses.

'Dream on Gail, you stupid cow! The Penny wouldn't associate with the likes of us,' Rita snaps. 'Tracy might get it off with her. She's got what it takes – as we all know.'

More laughter directed at Tracy. Gail persists in being helpful. 'We call the governor The Penny, Dee, short for Miss Pennyfields. She might interview you on Monday morning. This is what happens. You go into her office all scared and she sits there and makes you wait. The silence screws you up. I started blabbing about why I was sent down. She got to know everything she wanted without having to open her mouth.'

That's all right if you're guilty, Dee muses. She's not impressed with the prospect of standing on the mat in front of this Penny woman as though she's done something wrong. Doctor Tupman's slighting treatment has set her back up. The information about the governor's tactics is not new to her. She taught in a school where Miss Fletcher, the headmistress, operated in the same way. If Miss Fletcher knew that parents were likely to pose a problem, she kept them waiting outside her office to take the wind out of their sails. Dee's glad the inmates have warned her about Miss Pennyfields. She has time to prepare before Monday and a possible meeting with this official. How she's going to cope with the prisoners is a different matter.

Tracy's stare is intimidating. It will not do to show fear. Dee has already reached the conclusion that she must appear resolute, even if she doesn't feel it. It's easy to be a fierce mother when her kids are in trouble but can she be fierce in her own defence? She sits in the recreation room until bedtime. Inmates drop by to satisfy their curiosity and then move away. A woman called Bridget is friendly. She's a heroin addict, drug dealer. She looks dreadfully thin and haggard and makes Dee feel even more ignorant. She sends up a silent prayer of thanks that the undergrads at University only persuaded her to smoke cigarettes, not dope. Would she have refused?

The radio plays pop music from the charts. Every now and then the girls hum or sing along. When they hear a tune they know and like, there's a chorus of raucous voices. *Those were the Days my Friend,* Mary Hopkins sings, and so do the prisoners. There were certainly better days in my life than this one Dee reflects, better days in the lives of all these women. The words make her sad. Thea and Maddy like this song.

Mary Burns wanders over to Bridget.

'You okay this evening Brigitta? Gotta a new pal?' She drops her voice to an undertone. 'Do me a favour? Let Livesey know what she's in for with Manners, she's not street wise.' She moves off as though she hasn't spoken.

'She has to watch her back,' Bridget says. 'Her lover's a protective bitch. You'd be the one to get your eyes poked out if she caught you making up to Mary.'

'There's no chance I'll be making up to Mary!' Dee whispers indignantly. 'Where I come from we have women friends, we don't make a habit of getting into bed with them. Prison doesn't have to change that. Why does Mary bother with a lover that's dangerous?'

'You are green aren't you? The field's somewhat limited in here and I warn you, prison can change a lot of things. Noreen's her cellmate. She isn't all bad, her heart's in the right place. She went for her father when he attacked her mother but she didn't know when to stop. He fetched up in a wheelchair. She's quite a looker, that's her over there.'

Dee sees Noreen standing with her arm round Mary's waist. She's a large woman, black and beautiful – not a woman Dee would choose to argue with. She shivers.

'You're in for murder aren't you?' Bridget says. 'Room 15, Tracy Manners and her dyke followers. See what you make of that setup. You'll need your wits about you with Tracy as a roommate, that's what Mary wants you to know. Try not to cross Tracy. Go along with what she wants and keep yourself in one piece.'

'Why? What is she in for?'

'GBH. Hit her lover over the head and put her in intensive care. She's a tricky customer. Try to keep on the right side of her. She's a sexy bitch, just hope that's the worst you'll experience in her company.'

What a predicament – learning about the lives of these women while her own life is in peril. Dee watches the minutes tick away and when the end of session bell rings, she makes her unwilling way to Room 15. She and Tracy are checked in and the door is locked.

Dee likes to wash before bed. Tracy lets her go first and she's obliged to do her "face and fanny" bedtime ablutions in front of her cellmate. She's relieved to see that Tracy keeps her face averted until she's finished. Perhaps her cellmate isn't as predatory as she implied. By the time she gets into her bunk, her nerves are so taut that she feels sure she'll never be able to get to sleep. "Lights out" is called. There's enough dim light to make out the objects in the cell. Now she can think over this awful day.

How are her children? Her mum will have put Maddy to bed. They'll have looked out of the window at the yellow field of mustard seed rape and watched the sun set over Shawcross Woods. Maddy will have insisted on, *The Three Billy Goats Gruff*. Will Thea have been tucked up in bed with a goodnight story? Her eyes brim with tears. She wants to be there for Thea. Damn this hateful separation from her serious little daughter.

Her cellmate has no intention of leaving her alone with her thoughts. She drops down silently and sits on the edge of Dee's bunk.

'Let's get to know each other shall we? Two single females in one room. What shall we do?'

'We could go to sleep.' Dee whispers. 'From what I've seen of your activities, it looks as though you need the rest to keep up with your daytime pursuits.'

Tracy chuckles.

'Those three aren't serious girlfriends. They're what you call "jail turn outs" same as in America. You wouldn't catch them having sex with a woman if they were on the outside. They'll be back with men as soon as the prison doors shut behind them. I play around with them. Take advantage of the situation. I've always been into women.

'I had a lover but I blew it, clouted her over the head with a cast iron frying pan and put her in intensive care. Part of me thinks it was justified really because the bitch was having an affair with a bloke. If she'd told me, it might have been all right. Well... we might have parted under circumstances that wouldn't have landed me in here. The first I knew about the affair was when I saw him sneaking out of the back yard. But I know damn well that I've got a vicious temper when I'm roused. They've made me have sessions with a shrink while I'm here. Don't do anything to make me mad Livesey and we'll get on okay.'

'I'll do my best to keep out of your hair,' Dee says and she means it.

'You know you're quite a dishy woman?'

'Thanks for the compliment. I wasn't aware that you were weighing me up.'

'I weigh up every woman that comes into the Wing. I fancied you as soon as I saw your "scared little woman" look when Grundy showed you in. You looked dead comical batting about with the "dyke" information.'

'You didn't give me the impression that you liked anything about me.' Dee wants to ward off Tracy's too-interested line of approach.

'I have to keep up my sexy image when I'm with the girls. Startled you didn't it? But I'll tell you what Livesey, I liked what I felt when I pulled you to me.' She waits to see if Dee's going to say anything but Dee knows she's in dicey territory.

'Come on Livesey,' Tracy urges, 'I'm getting cold out here. Move over and let me in.' Dee opens her mouth to protest but Tracy claps her hand over it. 'Don't make a sound,' she hisses.

'You'll have the warders in here. I warn you, if there's trouble I'll say you started it. Come on relax woman. We need to see whether we're going to enjoy our nights together, if we're sexually compatible and all that. And don't pretend you're surprised Livesey. I bet you've fantasized about a scene like this when you've been masturbating. Innocent victim locked up with randy prisoner, forced to submit to her advances. Your fantasies won't ever be the same again Livesey. This is reality.'

And her hand is inside Dee's nightshirt.

She's trapped! She can't shout out and if a struggle is heard, she'll be the one who ends up getting hurt and in trouble. She's seething, a furious mix of anger at the abuse and helplessness in the face of it. Worst of all, Tracy fondles and kisses her breasts and her body betrays her. Her sad body, frozen after months of rejection from Jon, is suddenly invaded by this woman. Tracy owns it, sweeps her hands over and under, ignoring Dee's objections. She strikes fire in sensitive places, melting Dee's resistance and laughing because she gasps – her body, that has a will of its own to be loved. Her mind fights to resent the importunate fingers but her body sucks them in, riding and plunging them deeper. Her mind gives up the battle. The woman knows she needs, knows better than she does herself what she needs. She works with her, in her, until Dee begins to drown in sensation. She wants to scream at the release into orgasm and buries the sound in the warmth of Tracy's throat.

'Well, well, well! I am surprised Mrs, "I can't make up my mind whether I'm a lesbian or not." Travelled this way before have we? Fancy that! Who would have thought it? Mm. Responsive cunt, lots of nice times in Room 15 for Tracy Manners and Dee Livesey in the next three months.'

Dee turns her face away. She hasn't had a woman make love to her before but she's not going to say so. She's played into Tracy's hands. The unavoidable situation was created for her and she didn't know how to escape. She's even been a willing contributor. From now on, it will be twice as difficult to maintain an aloof exterior. She hopes sleep will provide an escape from her overturned world.

Saturday 9th May

Dee wakes long before the rising bell and tiptoes to the toilet. There's no movement from the upper bunk. She lies still, rigid with apprehension about the day ahead.

She's only one of many innocent women prisoners throughout history and there's no hanging or burning at the stake, to dread – not that lifelong imprisonment is a palatable option. She's not condemned by association because of a guilty male partner, as in the American drug cases, nor has she dabbled in herbs from the hedgerows and offended a male doctor, as in mediaeval times. She delivered the correct dose of Sodium Amytal to her mother-in-law and did her best to make an old woman happy. How can she prove her innocence?

It's not safe to let her thoughts dwell on Thea and Maddy, frustration makes her cry. Her children are both in the care of loving relatives. They can come on visiting days and three months will pass. She disguises an involuntary sob with a little cough. No one inside must know that she's vulnerable where her children are concerned, least of all Tracy Manners. From now on her expression must be permanently guarded and watchful. Let her fellow criminals be unsure as to whether she is capable of murder.

And last night, the sex, the darkness, the intimacy, and she came – she actually had an orgasm brought on by another person. Did that mean that she wasn't frigid? After the loss of her virginity that first time, when Jon said, "Nothing happened that time, perhaps it will next," she wondered what was supposed to happen. No wonder her pals at Uni said she was the most naïve person they'd ever met. It was much later that she learnt the word orgasm; it wasn't a topic of conversation among her friends. Until last night she believed she was a sexual failure and thought that was why Jon needed other women. Did they obligingly orgasm for him? Whatever the reason for last night, sex in prison with a woman succeeded where a man's penis failed.

She and Jon had reproduced, fulfilled the main purpose of marriage, and that was evidently supposed to satisfy her. The "love and honour" and "keep you only unto her," had gone by the board. But one night in prison, in bed with a woman, had shown her that sex can be amazing. She hadn't thought about the fact that a woman was most likely to know how to appreciate a woman.

Last night she fell asleep feeling guilty and ashamed, excusing her enjoyment in sexual pleasure by reasoning that it was a situation she couldn't avoid. This morning she's content to take her own pleasure from the incident.

Tracy's predatory approach has roused long buried resentment – memories of having to hide the sexual interference of her headmaster and grandfather from her mum and dad. This time she's defiant not cowed. Bridget's warning, about prison changing a person, is already proving to be true.

Dee is unsettled, outside her own field of experience and rules of behaviour, and with no guidelines for life in prison. She feels disconnected from her normal standards, as if she's a gate that's been lifted off its hinges. How to hold on to her integrity? Does integrity mean anything in prison? Should she care?

Hopefully, she won't be in the same work detail as Tracy, which will avoid daytime contact. She's not likely to see her again once she leaves prison. It won't be difficult to reject the whole, "sex with a woman thing," when she's released.


The rising bell rings and room doors unlock. Groups of prisoners file out to the showers. Dee copes with this introduction to prison routine by watching and following on. Tracy takes steps, she's close behind. She sees Rita mouth, "Did you?" and Tracy answer, "Yeh." Dee doesn't miss Rita's spiteful look in her direction.

The showers are communal. Her body is well soaped by willing hands, noticeably in the breast and thigh area, without being seen by an Officer. She's not sure how she's supposed to react. If she objects might she be punched, so she stands and lets it happen. It's not an unpleasant sensation to have soapy hands smoothing over her curves. She's living out one of her fantasies, although she'd always imagined a man servicing her in this way. There's never any of this sensuous behaviour with Jon. They never bathe together. He disappears into the bathroom and closes the door. She's surprised that the officers on duty don't know what's going on – or do they – and look the other way? Are some of the officers lesbians?

What does make her mad is her breakfast tray. Tracy's instructions to the cook have resulted in meagre portions. Dee feels her eyes blaze, her gut tense. The reaction surprises her. She grips her tray in an attempt to hide the fact that the sudden emotion has made her tremble. She sits down and eats the food without a word. Let them see that she's fuming. She'll smoulder and keep the malicious bitches wondering.

Tracy is mean. It wouldn't have harmed her to revoke her instructions to the cook. She had her own way in bed last night. She could have let her off this diet. As well as being violent, she's obviously a taker and a control freak.

Dee notices Mary make a wide detour from the serving hatch so that she passes their table. She sees the fingers of Mary's left hand wave a greeting from underneath her breakfast tray. Dee moves her head in a nod that's only perceptible to Mary. It's comforting to have someone make an effort to cheer her up. She wishes she could smile her appreciation.

Dee is detailed to work in the laundry on an easy sorting job, shirts to be piled in sizes ready for each wing. She likes sorting. As a mother of young children she's had plenty of practice with Lego blocks, beads and jigsaw pieces and making sure that board games are kept intact – then there's always the endless pairing of socks. With this job she doesn't have to talk to anyone.

Officers are in and out of the laundry the whole time but there are nice sneaky moments when the girls sing or perform a little routine to the music on the radio. *Obla Di Obla Da* sets them off but "the trusty" threatens to switch off the music. They groan good humouredly but the minute "the trusty" goes out of the room they act up. *I'll never Fall in Love Again* they sing into their imaginary microphones. Dee wholeheartedly echoes the sentiment. She's very interested in the "don't care" attitude to authority, actually finds it refreshing. Does condemnation and imprisonment free one to behave as one likes – matters couldn't be worse so why bother? *Lilly the Pink* has the girls dancing round in a line, "conga style". She declines their, "Come on Livesey" invitation. It would mean lowering her guard. She learns later, that one of the girls hit an old woman over the head with a brick and killed her and "the trusty" knifed her husband – prison is a fearful place.

The afternoon is the worst time. Caged, desolate women wander about aimlessly. Dee hides her tears and battles with despair.

In the evening the atmosphere's more relaxed. The Saturday night radio plays an early evening hour of ballroom dance music in the recreation room. 'Shut the bugger off,' and 'change the fucking station,' are desultory shouts, but no one obliges. Dee notices that two of the women hold each other close and smooch to every tune. A few women dance a half-hearted, silly Barn Dance round the table. Gail pulls Dee up from her seat and they join in. Noreen and Mary fit into the Barn Dance and Mary shouts loudly, 'Progress! Men forward, lady drop back!'

'Saw you were dancing man and it's a legit way to speak to you,' she whispers as Dee is her next partner. 'You okay?'

'I'm not short on new experiences.'

'Freak you out?'

'Not exactly,' Dee admits with a grin.

'Good for you.'

'Were you by any chance brought up on Chapel socials as you're au fait with this kind of dance?' Dee asks.

'How d'you guess?'

'I recognise the call – that's where I learnt to do ballroom dancing.'

Mary drops back to her last partner before the dance ends. When the announcer introduces a Quickstep, Tracy pushes in and grabs Dee. She clasps her in a sexy, hip grinding hold.

'Never mind fraternising with these other women,' she says menacingly, – 'fucking well stick with me.' The two of them demonstrate a very sexy bump and grind Quickstep.

Dee doesn't recognise the Officer on duty. She's elegant. Good figure, high cheekbones and short, stylish, ash blonde hair. The white uniform shirt suits all the officers.

'Who's that?' she asks Bridget.

'Officer Morgan, deputy governor, she checks up on all the wings but usually ends up in here, you'll see why.'

Officer Morgan stays to watch.

'Are you coming to dance?' Gail shouts across to her. Officer Morgan shakes her head.

Dee invites Bridget to do the *St Bernard's Waltz,* despite the fact that Tracy won't be pleased.

'I see you survived your first night,' her partner says.

'The advice you gave was the only option. Tracy doesn't allow for choice.'

'You're learning. At least you're here to tell the tale and not in the prison infirmary.'

'That bad?' Dee shudders.

'Can be... You dance well.'

'Thanks. I'm used to taking the lead after teaching hundreds of kids their first ballroom dancing lessons.'

'You're a teacher. What do you teach?'

'English, art, games, dance and drama and it's, "what did I teach?" I haven't worked for seven years. I stopped when I was pregnant with my first daughter Thea.'

'I think Mary was hoping to be a teacher. I know she was at University before she was sentenced.'

'Do you know why she's here?'

'Some accident with a student in her digs, the woman died. Mary got five years for manslaughter. They might shorten the sentence for good behaviour if she keeps her nose clean.'

'She seems really nice.'

'She is really nice but she has to play it cool in here, keep in with the lesbian crowd, they don't like her being clever.'

They sit down when the dance ends. Officer Morgan is grilling Tracy and she doesn't look very pleased. She keeps glancing over in Dee's direction. Tracy is answering the officer's queries in her nonchalant fashion but her questioner is in earnest. They must have come to some agreement because the Officer strolls off down the corridor with a backward look at Tracy.

'Watch this,' Bridget says.

Tracy has a quick word with Gail but she can't hide the fact that her eyes are on the corridor. She disappears in that direction.

'They're as thick as thieves,' Bridget says. 'Manners is more than happy to give Morgan what she wants. In return Morgan lets her queen it over everybody.'

'Tracy must have an amazingly capacious libido.'

'You've cottoned on to that one quickly.'

'Anyone that takes her attention away from me is welcome,' Dee says with feeling.

She hopes that Tracy might be satisfied with her sex with Officer Morgan and leave her alone. It seems likely as "Lights out" brings no figure dropping down on to her bed. She wakes to hear a clock strike midnight and tiptoes to the toilet. It's an unfortunate move on her part. Her sleepy roommate follows suit and pursues her to bed. She curls up behind Dee, cups her hand over her breast, grunts her approval and falls asleep.

Dee lies awake, squashed up against the wall, resenting the discomfort. She's hungry. If she'd been at home she'd have padded down to the kitchen to brew a pot of tea and eat some biscuits. Her favourite place is in the kitchen, where she sits on a step stool with her back against the Rayburn. But thoughts of home are not comfortable. Is Jon's latest woman friend Sarah with him in their bed? Will Thea be upset by her daddy sleeping with another woman? It's a long time before she can let herself doze off.


## Sunday 10th May

Dee wakes to feel Tracy's hand caressing her breasts and brushing over her pubic hair. She always feels sexier in a morning but is not going to encourage this bed-mate. The talk about breasts has disturbed her and Tracy's breasts are tantalizingly near.

'Must go to the loo,' she says and climbs over her bed companion.

'Hope you appreciate your good fortune in having me as a roommate,' Tracy gloats. She sits on the edge of the bed. 'There's a service in the chapel on Sundays. If you go this morning you'll have chance to pray for forgiveness for your sexual improprieties in the presence of a very nice lady Reverend. "Oh Lord, I have sinned. I've let myself enjoy sex with a woman." '

Good fortune? Dee compares her home life with prison. At home there was innocence and a faithless husband. Here there is the accusation of guilt and good sex. The good fortune is debatable. No way is she going to think of the sex as sin. The rising bell rings in the corridor.

'In the light of improved relations,' she ventures, 'how about relaxing the embargo on my food Tracy?

'Ah...now that would be ceding too much too soon – got to keep you in line babe.'

Dee knows better than to protest, she daren't ignore Tracy's unpredictable temper.

The prison routine is different on Sunday. Dee avoids the chapel and morning service. Singing the familiar hymns in a quiet place would undo her self control. Being amongst endless noise and voices keeps her dissociated from her unhappiness. She can maintain a tearless desolation.

The weather is fine in the afternoon. Dee props herself against a wall and watches the scratch game of netball that's being played in the exercise yard. The play is rough. Her referee's whistle would definitely have shrilled at the deliberate foul that forces the Wing Attack to limp off the court. The team is not prepared to play one short and the organizer yells at her.

'Can you play?'

'I'm out of practice.'

'Get in here and do your fucking best.'

Dee finds that she's able to support the ball up to the goal circle at a satisfactory speed but she's glad that there are only a few minutes left to play. Her legs would have buckled under her if the game had gone on any longer. She's puffed and hungry and can only expect the enforced diet at mealtime.

In the evening there are out-of-date magazines in the recreation room to leaf through. There's always music on the radio. Perhaps because it's Sunday the girls sing wistfully, *I was Born under a Wandrin' Star*. Dee sees more than one woman wipe her eyes when *Bridge over Troubled Water* is played. She and Bridget chat. There's no sign of Tracy. She daren't go to Room 15 in case she's there. She must wait for compulsory bedtime.

'Saved you this from teatime,' Mary Burns says in a quiet voice. Dee feels a hand on her shoulder and a biscuit is slotted into her pocket. 'I have to inform you that my middle name is Helen, not to be confused with the Helen Burns in *Jane Eyre*. It is unlikely that there will be an opportunity for you to show your gratitude for this small mercy, or join me on my deathbed.'

Dee smiles at the literary joke. Mary Helen Burns would be a nice friend if only they could find time to talk.

Her bunk is invaded after "Lights out." She moves over resignedly to make room but can't help saying, 'Oh no,' wearily.

'Oh yes, bitch. This is what I've been looking forward to all day. Once we're locked in, we do what I want. Get your nightshirt off.'

Tracy is undeterred by her cell mate's lack of response.

'New tactics tonight babe, see how you like muff diving,' and she disappears under the covers. Dee tries to stifle her involuntary shriek. But once again the sensations are more than she can withstand and she's transported along this fast track to orgasm.

'You've got me roused girl, now it's my turn,' Tracy insists. 'Play with my tits.' She rides vigorously to her own satisfaction on her cell mate's thigh.

When Tracy is asleep, Dee admits her unease. Tracy is a good looking woman, but the two of them have nothing in common. She's a bully and not someone Dee could be friends with. Unless Tracy is making love, she's a constant menace. "Stick with me," she says and, "this is what I've been looking forward to." Does she assume that they're a couple? She snuggles up in bed like a child expecting comfort. Is she becoming emotionally attached to her? Has letting herself respond to the sex been a terrible mistake? What will happen if Tracy wants affection and she can't give it, what then? Look what happened to her partner. Surely, when this woman's on the receiving end of admiration from so many prisoners, she doesn't need her cellmate in any capacity other than for sex.

Dee is aware that Tracy's sycophants dislike her. Tracy is a woman they adore, possessively. They pump Dee for information, try to find out what's going on, but she adheres to her non-communicative, vigilant state during the daytime. As far as she's aware, Tracy is not forthcoming about what they do once the cell door is shut. Her admirers are suspicious and jealous. Only three nights and already a frightening tangle threatens. She wonders if she'll meet the Prison Governor in the morning and whether her fears will be relieved.


## Monday morning 11<sup>th</sup> May

A frosty faced Officer Morgan collects Dee from laundry-duty at ten o'clock. Dee reckons from the sour look on the officer's face, every time they come into contact, that she's incurred displeasure by being Tracy's roommate. She's marched through the sequence of locked doors and up a flight of stairs. Dee glances into a room with SECRETARY on the door and sees a woman busy typing. Officer Morgan taps on the next door. Dee reads the name-plate GOVERNOR J PENNYFIELDS and thinks "nice name" before she's thrust into the office and Officer Morgan departs. There's silence.

It's a dazzlingly sunny room. Dee can't really see the governor. She's just a seated form bent over the papers on her desk, presenting a very attractive head of curly blonde hair to Dee's inquisitive eyes. Gail's information about the governor's interview technique has prepared her for this reception but it doesn't prevent a surge of disapproval. The woman is rude. Two can play at the silence game. She turns her back on the desk and its occupant and studies her surroundings.

It's warm and pleasant in the room, not at all the ambience one would expect to find in a prison. She admires the large rug in a rich red colour with an interesting border, 1930's type design. It covers most of the room. She bends down to touch it and is not surprised to feel that it's wool. Curiosity makes her wonder what the curtains are like and whether they co-ordinate. She moves over to the window. Walking about in this carpeted room is a pleasure after the awful echoing corridors and cells of the last three days. The curtains are pale gold material, with a pleasing red pattern at eighteen inch intervals, Rennie Mackintosh style. The combination is not just successful, it's delightful.

But moving to the window is a mistake. The two large Victorian expanses, on either side of the Governor's desk, let in the blaze of sunshine and face a view beyond the prison walls. Her breath catches in a sob and she leans her forehead against the frame. The distant hills are green, the sky is blue. Here and there she can see the purple of lilac and the white of hawthorn blossom. Down below, on the prison forecourt, there's an unkempt patch of ground. She feels the flash of gut-anger again. Beauty, freedom, her own home and garden denied to her by a false accusation. She's hungry. She's tired. She's weary with trying to keep her head in control of the tense situation and with lack of sleep. She hunches her shoulders and sticks her hands in her pockets.

There are two reproduction paintings in gold frames on the far wall. She's familiar with the Sargent on the left of the door, has always admired the enchanting composition of two girls in frothy white dresses lighting their lanterns against a background of flowers. The other painting is a Gainsborough portrait of his two daughters as they chase a butterfly. Two paintings of sisters, – are they of particular significance to the woman at the desk? To Dee they represent her two daughters and her cheeks are once again damp with tears. She jumps when she hears Governor Pennyfields speak.

'Do you approve of the paintings?'

The woman spoke first, Dee clocks up a minor triumph. She can't answer immediately and when she does it's obvious that she's choked with emotion.

'Very much, *Carnations, Lily, Lily, Rose* is a favourite of mine. It's just that the Gainsborough is too poignant for me this morning. I was snatched away from my daughters last Thursday and the prospect of three months without them is hard to bear. When is visiting?' She keeps her back to the governor.

'For you it will be a week on Wednesday. I see from your notes that your elder daughter is old enough to visit. Dorothea, unusual name, – are you by any chance a George Eliot fan?'

'Why, are you?'

'Very much so, but not *Middlemarch; Mill on the Floss* is my favourite.'

'Mill on the Floss has too sad an ending for me. You express your opinions in a very nice voice if you don't mind my saying so,' Dee says and feels enough in control to turn round and face the governor – who looks somewhat surprised at the personal remark. 'I know...I shouldn't make personal comments. My mother attempted unsuccessfully to instill that into me...but I'm interested in voices and yours is beautiful.'

Voices do matter to her. This woman's voice is rich and cultured. Jon's voice is deep and intriguing and his laugh is charming. Jon is charming... She wonders what Governor Pennyfield's laugh is like, not that she'll find out this morning.

The governor leans back in her chair and Dee finds she can't look away from the blue/grey eyes that study her. They're lovely, as is the woman's face. Neither of them speaks. At length Dee breaks her gaze, confused by the feeling that she could stare at the woman forever. It's all so odd! She's spoken to her as she would to a friend. How is she supposed to behave? Perhaps she should have waited for the governor to begin the conversation and not have made the personal comments.

'Look, if you've really too much work to interview me,' she says, 'could I please sit down and have a few minutes' rest in that wing armchair? I'm so tired. If you look at it from my point of view, I can't make matters worse if I take my chance with you,' – she accompanies the request with a wistful grin

Governor Pennyfields checks the pile of papers in front of her. 'Twenty minutes and then I'll be ready.' Dee knows she's being granted a favour. She slips off her sandals and curls up in the red leather chair. She must have fallen asleep because the next thing she hears is Officer Morgan's sharp voice.

'Livesey wake up.'

There's a cup of coffee and a Digestive biscuit on a side table near her chair. She eats the biscuit hungrily, and enjoys the coffee, but the return to the present is too harsh. She can't bear it. The few comfortable minutes have undone her resolve to master her feelings in front of this woman. She sobs and wonders how much more weeping she'll do before this prison sentence is over. She fishes about blindly under the chair for her sandals.

'Mrs Livesey, come and sit facing me,' Governor Pennyfields says firmly. Dee brushes the back of her hand across her face to wipe away the tears. A box of tissues is pushed toward her and she scrubs her face dry.

'Mrs Livesey, I have to ask you some questions.'

She hears the click of a recording machine. The serious business is about to start.

'Mrs Livesey, are you guilty?'

'Haven't you read my statement?'

Her rude answer is weighed momentarily but there's no change in the manner of the governor's address. 'I read statements after I've interviewed a prisoner and come to my own conclusions.'

'I like that,' Dee says quickly, anxious to prove that her curt reply is not her normal behaviour. 'I never used to read the report on a new pupil unless I met with a problem.'

'Are you guilty?'

Dee hesitates before answering the direct question. 'I haven't been believed to date and there's no guarantee that you're likely to believe me. A straightforward, "no I'm not guilty" is probably futile. I need to know whether you're disposed to believe what I say.'

'Why do you ask?'

Dee smiles whimsically and says, 'Let's go on posing questions and coming to no conclusions.' But governor Pennyfields has a job to do. She waits for an answer.

'I suppose, because I've had experience of telling the truth and not being believed. My primary school headmaster applied his disbelief to get me to show him my genitals. Here I am, twenty-three years later, banged up in prison because a detective doesn't believe me. That's why I ask. Telling the truth is no use unless the listener is disposed to believe it – though I realise that it must be well nigh impossible to distinguish innocence from guilt – unless a person is really well known – or there's a mound of justifying evidence. I often read a newspaper column where the apprehended person swears he or she is not guilty. I pick up the paper, weeks or months later, and find out that the person lied.'

'It says in the police report that you precipitated your mother-in-law's death. Did you?'

'I wouldn't have dreamt of harming Grandma Livesey,' Dee replies heatedly. 'I nursed her through two bouts of pneumonia and tried my damndest to make her feel comfortable and at home.

'I didn't like her being there,' she's determined to be honest. 'You see, my granny came to live with us when she was too old to live alone and I thought that was what families were supposed to do. I know I worried Grandma Livesey. I'm sorry about that. For months, I suspected that Jonathon, my husband, was in love with another woman and eventually I told her. I should never have done that. She idolized him, prided herself on the academic prowess of her family.' Dee allows herself a tight smile. 'I was tolerated as the capable mother and housekeeper.'

'What happened last Tuesday?'

She's relieved to hear this question. The governor is listening.

'I put my daughters to bed and was ironing in the kitchen. There was a knock on the front door. A very agitated young man was standing on the doorstep – he said, "There's an old woman lying on your front lawn." It was Grandma Livesey. I was horrified. I called to my husband Jon; he was in his study. I lifted her up, carried her into the living room and laid her on the sofa. I shouldn't really have moved her. I thought she'd just fallen and I'd better get her inside, off the damp grass.'

Dee remembered the weight of her limp mother-in-law in her arms. She'd been a tall slim woman, like her son, but the years had seen her shrink and her back curve. Dee used to trim her springy white hair and see that she took an interest in her clothes. That was all over.

'Jon phoned for the relief doctor. An ambulance was ordered. I ran upstairs to get Grandma Livesey's nighty and toilet things. That was when I saw the open window and called to the doctor to come up and look. It dawned on us both that Grandma Livesey had made her exit via the open window.

'I followed the ambulance in my car. Jon doesn't drive and somebody had to stay and see that Thea and Maddy were all right. I stood outside the Casualty Theatre and I could hear Grandma Livesey having her stomach pumped. That was when I realised that she must have taken an overdose.

'Jon was awful to his mother. I thought he might be happier, and our marriage would stand a better chance, if Grandma Livesey wasn't living with us. That was really stupid of me,' she says sadly. 'Jon isn't going to change. He's helped himself to other women throughout most of our marriage. Why would a change of accommodation for his mother help? The Health Visitor said it was the policy to move an elderly relative where possible, to prevent a family from breaking up. I went along with the Health Visitor's information but I didn't really know what to do. I was wretchedly unhappy.

'Last week, the Health Visitor sat upstairs and discussed alternative accommodation with Grandma Livesey. After that, Grandma Livesey wouldn't come downstairs. She kept to her room and I took her meals and tablets up on a tray. I didn't check whether she took the tablets. She must have saved them up so that she could take an overdose. Anyway, nothing I could have done would have comforted Grandma Livesey. She thought I was mad. She said so in the suicide note.'

'Yes, the suicide note...was there really a suicide note?'

'Oh yes. When Jon came up to Grandma Livesey's bed-sit he saw a white envelope on her TV. It was addressed to her nephew Fred. Jon read the letter. It said that she didn't want to move again and that I was mad. Jon burnt the letter in the Rayburn. Mad...' she says more or less to herself. 'That was unfair of Grandma Livesey after I'd tried so hard to make our home function happily. On the other hand, being here in prison doesn't make me feel very sane.'

'Go on.'

'There's not much more. I stayed at the hospital and the Catholic priest was kind. He said, 'Don't be taking all the troubles of the world on your shoulders m'dear.' He left a young priest to minister the last rites. Poor lad – it was a first time for the young man. He looked at me and said, "I think that's everything?" I couldn't help him because it was a first time for me too.

'Jon and I went to the hospital on Wednesday morning. Grandma Livesey was still alive. I wanted to see the Almoner. I suppose I was a bit crazy by then. I spoke vehemently. I said, 'Grandma Livesey must not come back to our home. We can't chance either of our little girls seeing a repeat of the suicide attempt. It's traumatic enough for us adults – for them it would be a lifelong horror.' We went along to Ward nine where Grandma Livesey had only briefly regained consciousness. She died while we were standing by her bed. That's it – that's what happened. The funeral's tomorrow.'

Dee buries her face in her hands. The funeral – and it's her wedding anniversary.

Silence.

'The poor woman,' Dee says wearily. 'I've been feeling angry because she attempted to kill herself after I'd taken care of her, but what must she have felt like to go to that extreme? I suppose it's my fault for trying to find a way out of the mess. Perhaps I deserve to be shut up in prison.' She feels drained and hopeless.

'There's one detail here in the police report that needs clarification Mrs Livesey. Sodium Amytal tablets, how do you account for the fact that too many tablets had been removed from the bottle?'

Dee can't prevent a smile. Her eyes crinkle with amusement. She can see Thea's startled look so clearly, – that day when her Grandma read the first paragraph of *Cinderella* four times. Her eyes were laughing then. She put her finger to her lips in a, "Shush, don't say anything," gesture to Thea. Her daughter slid off the arm of the chair in disgust and gave up on the story. She'd better give the governor the facts.

'When the tablets were first prescribed, my mother-in-law must have thought that, if she took more tablets than the recommended dose she would get better quickly. She appeared more and more confused. She said she'd seen Jon dressed in a pink velvet waistcoat and she and I had a good laugh – but Jon thought the time had come for me to administer the correct dose each day. I didn't check whether she took the tablets you see. I never wanted to insult her by assuming that she couldn't manage by herself. It was embarrassing enough to ask for her washing because she wasn't aware of urine smells.

'I admire her though, for being brave and acting as she did. She's relieved me from the trapped feeling I used to have when I heard her slippers tread across the hall-floor at ten o'clock every morning. She didn't go back upstairs till six o'clock in the evening. Jon doesn't approve of television but Grandma Livesey had a rented one in her room. I'm sure she looked forward to the evenings, I know I looked forward to mine.'

She's been rambling on. Surely there's nothing more the governor needs to know? She gets up and looks out of the window. 'I'm missing the lilac in my garden and the bluebells will be out in Parchester Wood. I like to take the girls for a picnic. There's no green here and all I can see down there is a miserable patch of untended ground.'

'The prisoners do the gardening,' Governor Pennyfields says. 'We can't allow them to work there because of the opportunity to run. You can see that the space is open to the car-park, the prison gates and all the vehicles that come and go.' She pauses. 'Have you any intention of running?' she asks suddenly.

'Where would I run to? No.'

'Would you be interested in rescuing that garden area?'

'I would! It's actually a forte of mine. I like the rescuing bit better than the chore of tending the garden afterwards.'

'I'll see that your work schedule is altered. You can start tomorrow morning.'

The governor's chair scrapes back and she walks over to the filing cabinet. Dee stares. What a handsome woman, tall with a figure as beautifully proportioned as her face! She didn't believe the girls but they're right.

'Oh wow!' She meant her appreciation to go unheard. The words are out before she can stop herself. The governor stands still and looks uncertain. The prisoner is between her and the alarm button on her desk. Dee is used to complimenting her pals and anyone whose appearance she admires, but a prison governor? She tries to cover her gaffe.

'Don't worry, it's just that the girls said you were gorgeous and I didn't believe that a prison governor could be anything other than plain and stern.' She grins mischievously but it appears that she's overstepped a boundary.

'What's so amusing?'

Dee doesn't answer. She can't. She's hoping that if she avoids the question it will go away.

'What a lovely orchid,' she says, and touches the petals of the Phalaenopsis on the office desk. 'Mine was in bloom when I left home but it's a darker pink than this. Don't you think that the fabric of a petal is one of the most...'

'What's so amusing?' She's cut short. The diversion didn't work.

'Oh, for heaven's sake, can't you forget it?' Her eyes must have betrayed her less than blameless thought. She actually thought that the governor's hips and breasts look shapely and sexy in the fitting navy skirt and crisp white blouse, but she can't tell her that. 'It's just something, something that I can assure you is inappropriate that crossed my mind.'

'What?' Governor Pennyfields has no intention of forgetting it. Dee panics. Her brain can never fabricate an answer but this morning she'd better make an effort. She isn't going to get away without an explanation. Is the woman a bit ego-sensitive? She runs her fingers through her hair in exasperation. Perhaps she can put it in context.

'The girls here consider that I'm very naïve and they're educating me. I'm familiar with some swear words. Now my vocabulary has been extended'. If she keeps up a torrent of words she might get away without telling the truth – though God knows why she's taking this particular roundabout route!

'I know the girls are showing off, trying to shock me. I've been called a posh cow, cocky bitch and various degrees of cunt and tits. I haven't met, hot ass and rumpie-pumpie before, nor do I use horny, shag and lots of the other words that are common practice in here. Is there a dictionary of slang in existence? I could extend my vocabulary. I'll check in the library.' Is she winning? No indication that she is. 'The other information the girls are passing on involves lesbian sexual behaviour. Lesson one was about appreciating a woman's breasts.' The woman's still waiting, she isn't satisfied. Damnation! It's the truth or nothing, okay. Dee accelerates her speech to get it over with quickly.

'I smiled because I looked at you and thought your breasts look beautiful in your crisp white blouse. It amused me because I've obviously learnt lesson one. Now can I go?'

The governor doesn't move or speak. Surely the woman can cope with a bit of flattery? Dee has had enough. 'I'll wait in the corridor,' she says. She opens the door before the governor has chance to object and lets herself out of the room.

Re-lived trauma and embarrassment, quite a session – she feels shaky after the interview. What an idiot she was, getting herself into such a fix. She won't have impressed the governor with her verbal diarrhoea, though the woman must be familiar with sexy talk. Not that Dee is used to it. Perhaps she's already lost her integrity.

There's no officer waiting. She hopes she can hang about on the landing and let the time pass until lunch. The interview concentrated on the immediate past. It didn't present her with an opportunity to air her concerns about Tracy Manners. Hopefully there's nothing dire on the immediate horizon. She leans her arms on the wide, polished, banister rail. It was pleasant in The Penny's sunny office. She'll call her "The Penny," now that she's seen her. "Governor," isn't personal enough for such a gorgeous looking woman.

She feels emptied of the rancour that had built up inside her but it was probably unwise to take the liberty of being pert, with someone who holds sway over her future. Maybe she's allowing the effect of Tracy Manners and Co to influence her behaviour. The whole situation is so extraordinary that she feels free to err on the outrageous side. The main question is – does The Penny believe her? Is she able to bypass the judicial system if she thinks a prisoner is innocent? She doubts it. Still, The Penny trusts her not to escape, and gardening is preferable to laundry work.

The governor's office door opens. She is not to be left alone. Out comes The Penny to supervise her. The clacking typewriter in the secretary's room stops. They're joined by a woman with a handful of letters. This woman isn't wearing uniform. She looks neat and efficient in a pink striped blouse and grey panelled skirt. Confronted by the unexpected contact with a prisoner, her pleasant expression becomes confused. She looks at each of them in turn. The situation amuses Dee.

'Dee Livesey, inmate 537, – how do you do? You must be Governor Pennyfields' secretary.' She offers her hand.

'Joan Carpenter, yes I am.' She shakes Dee's hand.

'I was admiring the Minton tiled floor down there,' Dee says to be conversational. 'My hall has a similar floor, on a smaller scale.'

'So has mine,' the secretary says.

'So has mine but on a larger scale,' The Penny adds.

They all smile. It's a nice relaxed moment. Does The Penny live in a mansion? The floor below them isn't small. Dee looks at the drop, they do too. She's in prison for allegedly having pushed her mother-in-law from a height. Their expressions indicate that the reminder occurs to the three of them simultaneously.

'I couldn't manage to heave the two of you over the banister rail,' she says and sets off down the stairs to join the Officer who is hurrying up to collect her.

Monday Evening 11ᵗʰ May

Dee joins the queue for the telephone and, with her face turned away from the waiting queue, so that no one will see if she cries, she catches up on the family news.

She hears that Maddy charmed the ladies at the chapel coffee morning on Friday. Her brother Robert came over on Saturday and took them all to feed the swans on Kingly Flash. Her sister Agnes and her husband John are driving up at the weekend. Thea is being well looked after by Jon and a lady called Sarah. Good, they're all rallying to help each other cope with the crisis.

'Get off the line Livesey. You've had your three minutes.'

'Bye Mum.'

She strolls along to the shop with her prison subs. Every one strolls in prison, there's no haste to be anywhere. Another minimal evening meal, thanks to manipulative Tracy Manners, makes her look longingly at the packets of biscuits but she's not ready for confrontation yet. She can afford to lose a few more inches. She buys a pad of notepaper and some envelopes. When all else fails, she's happy to lose herself in writing.

*My darling Thea,*

*I hope you found the birthday present I wrapped for Jill and had a good time at her party on Saturday. Have you moved on to the next reading book?*

*I'm okay. Would you believe that I'm wearing denim overalls? I'm going to work in a garden. Write to me please. I'd love to hear your news. I miss you very much.*

*Love from Mum XXXXXXX*

Writing the letter to Thea opens the floodgates. She rests her forehead on her hand to hide her face while she dabs at her eyes. She seems to be forever on the verge of tears! The second letter is to her brother.

*Dear Robert,*

*I'm glad you got over to Burylane at the weekend to give Mum and Dad a hand with Maddy.*

*There can't be a much worse situation for a family than this murder accusation. I can't see that we will ever live* it down. It's so awful that I'm numbed. I've ceased to be a person. I'm just 537 Livesey.

Maddy would be glad to see you. I hope she didn't ask too many unanswerable three year old questions. How I miss her cuddles!

*Write to me please.* Love Dee X

The third letter is to her sister and her husband.

*Dear Agnes and John,*

*Your sister is obviously not going to be famous for any of her artistic talents, just wretchedly notorious. I hope you're rising above the embarrassment and ignominy. I'm bewildered. However, there must be some intervention on the part of Angels or whoever, because it's as though there's a safety net over my mind which stops me from going crazy.*

*You will know John, from your experience in the Police force how desperate it is in prison. Have you heard of this Governor Pennyfields? She's a handsome specimen of authority! How's your garden? I daren't think about mine. Thankfully I've been given the job of rescuing a patch of ground here – it will get me away from everybody during the day.*

*Have a good trip up to Mum and Dad. Maddy will be pleased to see you. Poor Thea! I didn't know what to do. This Sarah is probably very nice and Thea won't go short of love but I miss the girls dreadfully, as you can imagine.*

*Lots of love and write to me please. Dee XX*

Her last letter is to her friend Charlotte.

*Hi Lottie,*

*I was so looking forward to your birthday party, baby sitter arranged and all. Toast yourself for me.*

*There ain't much fun in here!*

At this point the paper is snatched from her. Tracy and her cronies gather round. Tracy reads the few sentences and then, mimicking Dee and exaggerating her voice, reads aloud, 'There ain't much fun in here!'

'Not very good grammar, Posh Cow, and I thought we were giving you plenty of fun. Oh dearie dear! Fat Tits is not happy with us. She's going to be a fucking gorgeous shape with the diet we've got her on. Now why wouldn't she thank us for that?' She rips up the letter. 'Oh shit! Look what I've done. Now we'll have to write a happier one won't we? I notice you've been shopping Livesey. Don't think you can buy food to supplement your diet. I have my eyes everywhere in this Wing.' She and her sniggering crowd move away.

'Quite a different Tracy from the one that invites herself into my bed,' Dee mutters and thanks her lucky stars that she hid the other letters in her pockets. She hands them to duty Officer Parr.

'I'll leave these on Officer Morgan's desk,' Officer Parr says, – 'she deals with the mail.'

Dee hates relying on anyone to post her mail. She likes to see her correspondence safely disappear through the opening in the red pillar box.

Tracy returns alone and lounges in one of the armchairs; she looks lost without her group of hangers-on. Dee is conscious of being watched. What a miserable trait Tracy exhibits in persisting with this petty diet control. What good does it do her? Is she afraid of losing face with her buddies, particularly if she was to withdraw her instruction to the kitchen staff? Perhaps her numerous seductions get a bit meaningless after the first few dozen. Tracy is in prison because she's violent – no use trying to understand how she thinks. Dee directs a fearless look in her direction. Let the bullying prisoner be unsure about this particular worm.

# WEEK TWO

This is Dee's fourth day in the prison forecourt garden. It's been hard work. Officer Waering is assigned to her. She sees that her charge has the necessary gardening equipment at the start of the morning and afternoon work periods. She checks in the tools at the end of each session.

Officer Waering isn't as brisk as the other officers. She's more homely, with curly permed hair and a comfortable figure. She chats about her family. Her two boys are at secondary school. The younger one is driving her daft because his granddad has given him an old piano accordion and the walls of his bedroom are not very soundproof. The older boy is a railway engine enthusiast and spends his weekends at the train station, taking down numbers. Officer Waering's husband works for the Royal Mail. They don't get much time together as a family because of shift work. She asks Dee about her children but realises that it upsets her to talk about Thea and Maddy. They discuss their interests instead. Officer Waering's keen on gardening; her husband put up her greenhouse and constructs pathways and raised flowerbeds.

'You chose your husband wisely,' Dee says. 'I didn't think about practical matters when I fell in love. My husband Jon is an academic. He's good at knocking things down. He demolished the cronky old brick garage so that I could lay out another section of garden. I told Governor Pennyfields that I was used to garden rescue jobs.'

It's great to be working alone, to be outside and trusted not to escape – not that the idea would have occurred to her anyway. She can't believe that this remand sentence is likely to end in life imprisonment. Hateful though the experience is, it shouldn't last long if the defence lawyer is working on her case.

She pruned the overgrown shrubs on Tuesday morning and began the digging. Since then, she's turned over the whole patch of ground and freed it from weeds. The clods of earth are ready to be broken up with the rake. She surveys her handiwork and puts on her gardening gloves. What a beautiful morning!

'You've done well,' a voice says.

It's The Penny. Dee looks forward to seeing her. Sometimes she says, "Good morning," – at other times she doesn't speak, just examines the progress and heads for her office. Dee smiles with pleasure. She folds her hands on the top of the rake handle, rests her chin on them, and contemplates the cool visitor in front of her.

'You'll be ready for planting next week. Do you think roses would look well here?'

Dee wonders why The Penny isn't affected by the heat of the morning sun – she's sweating before she's started work. The Penny's so handsome in uniform, captivating. It's a treat to stand and admire her. A newspaper photograph of Ingrid Bergman was the last woman's image she fell in love with, she could easily transfer her affections to The Penny's image.

'Wake up Mrs Livesey, roses. Do you agree that roses would look well planted here?'

'Yes roses,' she must concentrate, – 'roses erm...yes. Can we plant mainly fragrant varieties and I don't like lots of bare soil in between rose bushes do you? Shall we fill the spaces with perennials? At home I have Day lilies, Japanese anemones, Pyrethrum, Rudbeckia, Astilbe and Helenium because they spread, and carry on flowering into late summer, whereas roses would be over by...' She runs a hand through her hair as it dawns on her – late summer – please God she won't still be here when the yellow Rudbeckia daisies are in flower. The Penny notices the unfinished sentence.

'Is something the matter?'

'It occurs to me that despite my free bed and board at Stonebridge, I would rather not be in residence when the late summer flowers are blooming.' The Penny inclines her head in acknowledgement but doesn't comment. 'What were we talking about?' She's finding it hard to concentrate on the garden, she'd like to chat with this woman, keep her here.

'We were choosing plants.' Is The Penny trying to hide a smile, enjoying her discomposure?

'Yes, that's right and it's May, warm enough for annuals, they'll give colour.'

'I'm sure that can be arranged.'

The Penny doesn't seem in any hurry to go. Standing in sunshine must be preferable to working in an office. It won't be possible for her to befriend prisoners, Dee thinks sadly. Not that there's anyone out here to observe her behaviour, but prison walls have windows. Dee watches her walk over to her parked car, a beautiful white Jaguar, and lift out her briefcase. She waves a bottle of sun-tan lotion and calls, 'Mrs Livesey, are you wearing protective lotion?'

'The System provides it,' Dee says, 'but I would much rather have worn yours.' She clutches her hands passionately to her chest and flutters her eyelids, no point in teaching drama if she can't act up on occasions. Her audience is not amused. She reaches inside the car again.

'Have you got a hat?'

'Alas, the System provideth not headgear.'

'It's too hot for you to work with your head unprotected… pestiferous woman.'

Dee hears her add the last words after she catches the large, floppy-brimmed cloth hat, tossed in her direction. Was she meant to hear that? What does she mean, pestiferous? She was only having a bit of fun but she's satisfied if it means she's got under the woman's skin.

'Ooh stripes! Debenhams, very classy, thank you.' Wow, wearing The Penny's hat! She pulls it well down on her head. 'Does it suit me?' she shouts, but when she raises the brim to look, The Penny is striding across the car-park in the direction of Reception.

Dee watches until she is out of sight and then sings, sotto voce at first.

*When I woke up this morning,*
*You were on my mind,*
*And you are on my mind…*

She feels light hearted. There's no one around who can hear, and she dances round the rake singing out loud.

> *I got troubles whoa-oh,*
> *I got worries whoa-oh...*

A movement attracts her attention. She sees Officer Morgan step back from a window on the ground floor. Has she been watching? Dee is already under fire from the jealous inmates, they call her Penny's Pet. There'll be trouble if Officer Morgan chooses to fuel the fire.

It was a one sided bit of fun. The Penny has much in common with Queen Victoria. Dee recognises that she wasn't just trying to amuse her – it was as though she was flirting with her. She looks up "flirting" in the Oxford Dictionary in the prison library. *To flirt: behaving as though attracted to someone, or trying to attract someone, but for amusement rather than with serious intentions.* Yes, in that case she's flirting with a prison governor. One wouldn't seriously set one's cap at a person in her position. She's probably married. She must remember to look at her ring finger the next time they meet. The governor is known as Miss Pennyfields but that could be her professional title. Dee feels playful in The Penny's company and is pleased that she can look out of her governor's office window and see Prisoner 537 at work.

Outside, she might have these blithe moments but it's a different story once she's back inside the prison walls.

Monday 18th May

The Penny's Jag is disappearing through the main gates when Dee arrives at her garden patch. She experiences a pang of disappointment. The prison seems bearable when she knows The Penny's on duty.

A second weekend has passed with only one unpleasant altercation in the library. A gang of prisoners took it into their heads to annoy her. Each book she took down from the shelves they removed from her grasp. "I was reading that." "Give that 'ere," "That one's too hard for you," – stupid interference until she walked out of the library to the sound of their triumphant jeers.

On Sunday she started her period and told Tracy.

'Doesn't stop us sleeping together,' Tracy said.

'I don't sleep well when I'm squashed up against the wall Tracy,' she dared to say. 'Let's sleep in our own bunks and we can resume activity, if you like, when my period stops.'

'You don't tell me what to do bitch,' Tracy snapped.

'Okay, as long as you don't mind me bleeding on you. I have heavy periods.' It wasn't true but it was worth a try. Tracy made no effort to sleep with her last night. Neither of them spoke. Dee was pleased to have her bunk to herself and weathered the pervading hostility.

Her despondent mood changes when she sees the plants that are waiting. Her instructions are that she's not to step beyond one metre from her plot. The plants have been placed inside the metre boundary. There are fifteen rose bushes and root after root of perennials, wrapped up and tied with twine. She looks curiously at those. The roses are tied with labels from Aston's Nursery but the other labels are cut out of cardboard and handwritten. Who has gone to all that trouble? Who has a garden with an herbaceous border that can spare so many roots?

She spends ages thinking about heights and breadths before planning a layout. It's not her garden. How does The Penny want it arranging, in straight lines, in semi-circles or groups? She could have done with her opinion. She's pleased that The Penny has confidence in her and decides on three groups of roses, with perennials in between. She starts digging holes and teasing out roots. How super to have so many plants. The prison must have a good budget or has the money come out of The Penny's pocket? It's not her business but she can't help thinking that The Penny's pocket must be well lined. Jags don't come at tuppence-ha'penny, soon to be 1p in February next year, when decimalisation is introduced.

Dee's latest mode of transport, a Morris Minor Traveller which she acquired for eighty pounds and painted puce-pink because she likes odd vehicles, would not impress The Penny. Being able to drive, that's something for which she's grateful to Grandma Livesey. It was money saved from her housekeeping that paid for her driving lessons. There were no motor cars in Dee's family so she had to start from scratch and went to car maintenance classes at night school. She failed her first driving test. Grandma Livesey was there, standing by the Rayburn, waiting eagerly for her news and encouraging her to go on and try again. She passed her third driving test and then took Grandma Livesey for outings. She must remember the good things.

Her garden wouldn't impress The Penny either, the little additions she's made. Roots and seeds donated by friends and an occasional purchase from the market or a nursery. She's learnt a lot from studying *Amateur Gardening* magazines – but she still makes her plants dizzy by moving them from one position to another, because she can't decide where they'll look best. She hopes that Jon has mown the grass.

The plants are watered in by tea-time and the plot looks good. She's left room at the front for annuals. She stands with her hands in her pockets feeling quite the gardener – even feels regret that she won't see the established garden in years to come. She quickly follows that thought with a fervent prayer that she will *not* see the garden in years to come.

Movement again at one of the windows – Officer Morgan peering out – she backs away when Dee catches sight of her. Officer Morgan is one disagreeable woman.

## Tuesday afternoon 19th May 1970

'No gardening this afternoon Livesey,' Officer Waering says after lunch 'You have a Prison Visitor waiting to talk to you.' Dee grimaces. 'No need to worry. It's normal procedure, particularly for prisoners on remand. It's a check on your welfare. We have to know as much about you as possible.' She takes Dee to ROOM ONE and introduces her as Prisoner 537 Livesey, to a woman called Frances Pointon. Dee leans against the closed door, unwilling to begin the interview. Her eyes wander round the room.

'The décor,' she says at last, 'would you describe it as a pale shade of mouldy cheese green?' The visitor smiles and motions Dee to sit on the other side of the table between them. Frances Pointon is older than any woman she's seen in prison so far. She's clearly familiar with, and in command of, this type of interview. Her manner is attentive and interested. 'Don't we need an officer in here to guard you, in case I'm aggressive?'

'I can assure you that an officer is never very far away,' the visitor replies pleasantly. 'I hope there will be no need for aggression this afternoon. It's too hot.'

'Do I call you Frances?'

'Yes, if I can call you Deanna.'

'I prefer Dee. You look cool and unofficial in your Liberty lawn Frances. I like that design but if it was on me I'd look like an overgrown flower bed.'

'You like Liberty fabrics?'

'I used to rave about them when I first started to sew my own clothes, before I had children. My husband and I used to rent a flat in London during the summer holidays, while he referenced material for his B.A. at the British Museum. I was supposed to be his amanuensis but I kept falling asleep. It was so quiet in the museum, and I wasn't particularly interested in the subject matter, so I went shopping on my own. Liberty's fabric department was my favourite destination. Do you know the leopard skin design, black marks on a tobacco coloured background? I made a super straight through dress in that fabric a few years ago, when I had a figure that looked good in that style.'

'Your figure looks pretty well in proportion to me.'

'I've put on inches since my daughters were born but I suppose I'll slim down now that the girls have forced me to diet.' She notices the recording machine.

'We have to record these interviews,' Frances says apologetically.

'Who listens to the tape?'

'Anyone involved with your case. What were you saying about your diet?'

She's not sure how much to tell this woman. Could she get information about her fears to The Penny by way of this tape?

'Does Governor Pennyfields listen to the tape?'

'Yes.'

'In that case I want her to know that my cellmate Tracy Manners has bullied me from the minute I arrived. She controls and insults me in every way she can. She's instructed her pals in the kitchen to cut my food rations, just for a whim as far as I can tell. I'm hungry all the time.'

'Have you reported this to anyone?'

'The only authoritative person who is in contact with us is the Deputy Governor, Officer Morgan.'

'You could report it to her.'

Dee can see that Frances is surprised by the look of scorn on her face. She has to explain.

'Officer Morgan is a close, intimately sexually close, friend of Tracy Manners. Neither of them would lift a finger to help me. I'm only coping with the semi-starvation by maintaining an apparently unconcerned exterior. I don't want them to see that their scheming affects me. I can afford to lose a few inches but I'm not sure how long I can carry on eating such small meals. Also...' she pushes herself back from the table. In the company of a kind listener she's losing control of her feelings. 'Let me just get up and stand around for a minute,' she says, her voice breaking. The misery refuses to be battened down any longer. She faces the wall and sobs, struggling to stop crying and regain her composure.

'Come and sit down,' Frances says gently.

'I haven't told you it all,' she gives Frances a watery smile. She wants to get rid of the whole story before it's time for the interview to end. 'On the afternoon I was admitted, Tracy Manners fondled my breasts in front of an audience of her sexual partners. She climbed into bed with me the first night, warning me that I would be punished if I raised the alarm. She's done the same every night since, either to have sex with me or just to sleep close to me. Another prisoner advised me to go along with whatever Tracy wanted because she would be dangerous if I crossed her. From the way Tracy speaks to me, I get the impression that she thinks I'm her property and sexual partner.'

'How does that make you feel?'

'Furious! I don't want to be Tracy Manners' partner! In my world, sex between women isn't talked about so I think I'm coping very well in the circumstances. What makes me mad is the way adults, male or female, assume they have a right to work out their sexual urge on somebody else. It doesn't seem to matter whether they choose a man or a woman.'

Frances listens carefully.

'Are you a counsellor?' Dee asks her.

'I was a Probation officer, I took early retirement'

'I'm embarrassed to say this. Even though Tracy's predatory, she's the first person to make love to me in a way that is wonderfully satisfying. I'm tormented because my body wants to enjoy the sex but my mind resents her – and the enforced situation. Isn't that contrary?' She runs her hands through her hair and gives a self deprecating laugh. She doesn't feel proud of this admission. 'Enjoyment and resentment, with a cellmate who has a harem and thinks she owns me.'

Dee senses that Frances is watching her closely because she's worked up. She bets Frances is thinking she might be capable of violence.

'I don't know if I can continue to keep calm in the face of all the insults from the prisoners. There's just one woman in here that is kind to me, Mary Burns. The trouble is, she's got a lover who won't let her out of her sight so there's been no chance to for us to talk. I've never hurt anyone in my life. If I was to lose my cool now and try to deal with Tracy it would substantiate the suspicion that I murdered my mother-in-law. I'm already lying awake at night, planning how I would defend myself if any of the prisoners attack me. That's why I want Miss Pennyfields to know what's going on. She could step in and prevent trouble. And there's a personal detail; I started a period this morning and I've banned Tracy from my bed. I get hardly any sleep when the two of us are squashed in together. She's not pleased. I'm told she's in prison because she harmed her lover. I daren't let my guard down for a minute.'

Frances assures Dee that the tape will be given to Miss Pennyfields.

'Miss Pennyfields…she's called The Penny in here. The girls are crazy about her.'

'What do you think about her?'

What an odd question! What does she thinks about The Penny?

'She's stunning to look at and I love her voice. She spoke respectfully at my interview which is good for any prisoner's self esteem and she didn't seem to resent my personal remarks. It was difficult to know how to talk to her. I refused to be the pathetic prisoner in her presence because I haven't done anything wrong but, while I'm in Stonebridge, I have to accept that she's authority versus my alleged culpability – which doesn't make for good conversation as you can imagine. I'm a naïve ex-school teacher, housewife and mother. She's a highly professional woman. Our lives are worlds apart. The day brightens when she's around.' Dee smiles her infectious smile. 'I've actually found myself flirting with her. She's so correct and detached. I can't get her to laugh. I want her to notice me as a person, and not think of me as a criminal. I suppose she can't do that while I'm in here, suspected of murder.'

'No, her position is very clear with regard to prisoners while they're in her care. It's difficult for you,' Frances appears to commiserate.

'You'd better wipe that talk about flirting off the tape Frances. You see, I don't know what's happening to me. The beliefs I've held all my life, about certain behaviour being wrong, are vanishing after a few days in prison. If my friends knew that I was tolerating, even enjoying sex with a woman what would it make them feel about me? Would they feel unsafe near me? Would they think I was after them? Oh Frances, I have plans to compartmentalize this prison experience and shelve it when I'm released.'

'That might not be easy.'

'I hope you're wrong. I'm bound to be more thoughtful and understanding about the lives of women, after listening to their stories. The girls introduce extraordinary topics. They asked me last night whether I felt more of a man than a woman. I'd never thought about it.'

'What did you say?'

'Well, I'm picking up their expressions, so I said that I was delightfully fem and beautifully butch. It's true that whatever I wear affects how I feel. I said for example, that long skirts and an evening at the theatre bring out the fem in me, and my bib and braces overalls emphasize the butch. They said I must be bi-sexual. Do I have to have a label? I'm a woman for heaven's sake!'

'Exactly,' Frances looks at her watch and removes the tape. She writes *Prisoner 537 Livesey 19th May 1970*. 'I'll see that Miss Pennyfields gets this.'

'I'm glad you were my visitor,' Dee says. 'It's been nice to meet you. What were we supposed to talk about anyway? Should I have attempted to convince you of my innocence?'

'Something along those lines,' Frances smiles.

Dee shakes hands with her. 'Do I get only the one visit from you?'

'Yes, unless you have any problems.'

'I think I've enough problems thank you but...it might be worth creating a few to get you back here.'

'Don't try it!'

'In that case I don't imagine I'll see you again.' Dee says regretfully.

'You never know...don't rely too much on that imagination of yours,' Frances replies.


## Wednesday 20th May

Dee is at war with greenfly and some obstinate weeds. Traffic is endless in the mornings, delivery vans, police cars, staff cars, lawyers, social workers. She doesn't notice The Penny's Jag until the boot makes a yawning opening sound.

'Good morning,' The Penny calls and begins to carry across trays of annuals. She's wearing a white T shirt and light blue shorts. Is it her day off? 'I was in the market and thought these would fill up the empty spaces,' she says. They read the labels, Nemesia, Petunia, Nicotiana, Lobelia, Antirrhinum and half a dozen Begonias. 'I thought this grey-green feathery foliage would set the flowers off nicely. What do you think?'

'These should make a lovely display,' Dee says with enthusiasm. 'It's a good day for planting. Rain has been forecast for tonight.' Then she looks at her. 'What on earth are you doing here if it's your day off? You look absolutely gorgeous as usual, Miss Pennyfields. You ought to take advantage of this fine spell of weather and be out in the country, with some nice company. Thank you for bringing the plants. I hope I'll arrange them to your satisfaction.'

She's deliberately dismissive. The casual dress is too vivid a reminder of her lost freedom, – the good quality clothes an uncomplimentary contrast with the lack-lustre, cheap clothes in her wardrobe at home. She watches the Jag cruise out of the gates. How lovely it would be to sit in the passenger seat of a car like that and go for a drive with The Penny. But would it? She has to do all the talking when they meet. Can The Penny chat? Has she a sense of humour?

She begins the grouping and planting of the annuals. She feels tired. Surely the lack of food isn't having an effect as soon as this? She hasn't been here a fortnight. She aches for Thea and Maddy and there's the strain of constant watchfulness when she's with the prisoners. Frequent jibes at mealtimes are a trial. "How's Penny's Pet today?" "I must try talking posh and see if it gets me anywhere." "Got your knickers off for The Penny yet?" To the latter, Tracy would snarl angrily, "She'd better bloody not," which made things worse. To Tracy's groupies, it was an indication that something was going on between Tracy and Dee once they were inside Room 15.

Dee isn't sure if she can hold out. Being on the receiving end of constant hostility is testing her reserve to the limits. If she answers back, or breaks down and cries, her tormenters will have won. She couldn't bear to have them lord it over her. One bully is more than enough.


## Wednesday afternoon 20th May

The third Wednesday of the month is Visiting Day. Dee has no idea whether any of her family will come. Her mum was uncertain about leaving Maddy with her dad. She said that, since the separation from her mother, Maddy won't let her granny out of her sight. Dee has made no effort to contact Jon. Thea should have had her letter. She expected her to write back, and John and Agnes. It isn't like them to let a week pass before replying.

Officer Parr collects her at two o'clock and steers her along to VISITORS' RECEPTION. She's shown to a table and told to remain seated. Officer Morgan is on supervision duty and patrols the room. Dee recognises a few of the prisoners who are already talking to their families. Tracy said she was hoping for a visit from her sister. She sees the two of them in earnest conversation. The sister is largely pregnant and looks careworn. Dee looks round for Mary Burns but there's no sign of her. Mary mustn't be expecting a visitor. Then she sees Jon and, despite everything, she wants to cry out to him for comfort. Thea comes running down the aisle and Dee slips from her chair and catches her in her arms. Jon sits down on the chair opposite.

'Livesey, back on your seat,' Officer Morgan orders. 'Put the child down.'

Dee is not willing to let go of her precious armful.

'Put the child down,' Officer Morgan says again.

Dee snaps. She's furious with Officer Morgan for telling her what to do with her child. She has no need to interfere and spoil the few minutes she's allowed with her family. Her eyes blaze but she controls her voice.

'My daughter's only here for a short time,' – she spits out the words. 'She's doing no harm.' She turns her back to Officer Morgan and sits Thea on her knee. She notices Tracy's head turn in her direction.

'Did you get my letter?' she asks Thea.

'No Mummy.'

'That's very odd, I wrote to you the first week I was here.' She looks enquiringly at Jon.

'No,' he says, 'no letter from you.'

'You see the shop over there Thea? Would you go and buy us a packet of biscuits to eat please?' Jon digs in his pocket for money.

'There's a bully limiting my food,' Dee says as soon as Thea is out of earshot. 'She's roomed with me and she's scary, not bad for sex though.' They smile at each other sheepishly. 'Joking aside, it's pretty hellish.' She draws in a sharp breath to control the tears of despair that well up in her eyes. She mustn't cry in front of Thea. 'Is Thea okay?'

'She's managing as well as can be expected. Dee I'm so sorry about the note Mother left, whatever was I thinking of to burn it? The bastards won't believe me. It's all so crazy! Everybody's been sending references, hoping to help, but God knows what else we can do to get you out of here.' They sit feeling bleak and helpless. 'Your mum can't make it today. She'll come next time. She says you're keeping in touch with her.'

'I phone her when I can. I haven't phoned you because I'd break down if Thea answered the phone and I wouldn't want to speak to Sarah. Get something organized before I'm released Jon... If I'm released.'

'Christ! You'd better be.'

Thea has chosen a packet of Jammy Dodgers. She and Dee sit eating them. The time flies. Mother and daughter cry as they hug goodbye. Jon pats Dee's hand comfortingly. 'Keep your hopes up.'

'Thank you for coming,' she whispers.

She tenses as soon as they've gone. In defying Officer Morgan she's thrown down the gauntlet. She expects retaliation. She's flouted Tracy's rules in her presence by eating biscuits. She anticipates trouble.

Nothing happens that night. Tracy maintains a disapproving silence.


## Thursday morning 21st May

'Behold your escort for this lovely morning,' a cheerful voice says and Dee is surprised to see Mary Burns. 'Officer Waering's held up in a traffic jam so yours truly has been appointed "trusty" to do the necessary. Now, show me what you've been up to.'

Dee is delighted to have a chance to be alone with her. The two women are similar in build, athletic, with well proportioned figures. Mary is the taller of the two. Her whole body exudes energy and lively interest. They talk animatedly as they examine the new flower bed. Dee answers Mary's queries about the plants and layout.

'Gosh! It's nice out here,' Mary says. 'I wouldn't mind this job. I'll put in for it when you leave.'

'When do you expect to be released?'

'Hopefully next summer, if I don't blot my copy book with some of these blasted inmates.'

'Would you tell me how you got sent down, if it's not too painful?'

'It is painful and I cry if I talk about it. Let's go into the shed.'

The shed is bathed in sunlight. They sit on the wooden floor in the shade of the back wall.

'I was in the autumn term of my second year at Leeds University, reading for a BSc,' Mary begins. 'I'd lived in hall the first year but we had to move into lodgings for the second year. A friend called Enid asked me to share with her. I didn't know she was a lesbian and fancied me. Her father told me later that she'd been "out" since she was seventeen. One afternoon, she came at me wanting a clinch. It was unexpected and I was dead embarrassed. I sort of playfully pushed her away. There was a stool behind her and it tripped her up. She staggered back and hit her head on the sharp corner of the mantel piece.' The tears pool in Mary's eyes and she clutches her stomach as though the pain is there. 'She was dead, I knew she was dead. I phoned for an ambulance and then I blacked out. I came to as the door burst open and the nightmare of ambulance men, policemen, university officials and parents began. I was taken into custody the same night.

'My father's a fundamental, born again Christian. He and my mother are very conservative and anxious to keep face with their friends and the congregation. Did you notice that I had no visitors?' Dee nodded. 'I've an uncle that visits when he can, my mother's brother. Enid's parents were okay with the fact that she was a lesbian. They were very kind to me in the circumstances. They knew Enid's death was an accident. But I've caused someone's death Dee. I can't get over the horror and I feel as though my life's ruined. I go over and over it in my mind. Why did it happen to me? I give one small push and someone's dead? You'd question the validity if it was written in a story, you know – fact stranger than fiction. Thanks for listening, it helps to talk. I think I need this time in prison, away from the outside world, to get my mind in gear and let the public forget about me. '

'Will you go back to University?'

'I don't think so. I enjoy reading. I might get a job and take some advanced level exams in literature or languages.'

'Will your parents support you?'

'They're comfortably off. They might fund a course of study, as long as they don't have to see me.'

'What?'

'It was unfortunate that Enid's dad mentioned to my parents that Enid was in love with me and wanted me to be her partner. That did it for Mum and Dad. They're ruled by fear of what people think. The only way they can cope with what they believe to be a lesbian criminal daughter is to cut her out of their lives. I'm in a lesbian relationship here, with Noreen. She's my cellmate and she's looked after me from the word "go". The girls wouldn't dare to cross her. You see, now that my parents have disowned me, their friends will sympathise with them. They'll be considered admirable for refusing to be tainted by association with a lesbian daughter. If they give me financial support, the gesture will earn them regard in their circles...kindness to a sinner earns heavenly points and so on. Sorry, that's bitter. But I'd rather work and provide for myself than accept help in those circumstances. I might get help from the government, rehabilitation of ex-prisoners and all that.'

'What about love? The love that parents say they have for their children? I can't imagine shutting my daughters out if they get into trouble. How could someone like your dad, who professes the love of Christ, cast you off?'

'They'd have coped with the accident and my prison sentence... just about,' she shrugs wearily. 'It's the lesbianism. To them I'm a homosexual criminal, perverted and abhorrent. We exchanged letters at first. I tried to get them to understand that lesbianism doesn't harm anyone. I explained that harmful actions are the ones that constitute perversion, but I could have been talking double-dutch.' She and Dee stand up. 'I suppose I'd better get back inside or they won't trust their temporary "trusty," she says with a resigned smile.

'Come here,' Dee says. She feels the two of them need the comfort of a hug.

A shadow blocks out the sunlight. Officer Waering has arrived.

'Hi Officer Waering,' Dee greets her. 'Mary has been telling me about how she came to be sent down and we were giving each other some mutual comfort.'

'I see. While the cat was away, the mice had a play. I'm absent for a few minutes and look what happens,' she says pleasantly, – 'now you'd better get on with some work or there'll be trouble.'

At the end of the morning there's a summons from the governor. An officer has been dispatched to escort her upstairs. Dee hopes The Penny has had time to listen to her tape and that her situation with regard to Tracy Manners will improve. She outstrips the accompanying officer on the stairs, in her eagerness to get to the interview. Her reception is like being doused with cold water. She narrows her eyes in disbelief as she listens to The Penny's tirade.

'You don't seem to realise Mrs Livesey that your work in the forecourt garden is a privilege. This morning I witnessed the abuse of that privilege. You allowed prisoner Burns to accompany you to the out of bounds location and detained her in conversation. You disappeared into the garden shed and remained there until Officer Waering arrived. I'm obliged to withdraw the privilege. You'll please return to work in the laundry as from this afternoon. You may go.'

Dee is so angry she can't move. What's bugging the stupid woman? She's not going to leave this room dismissed as if she was a naughty child. Her voice, when she can bring herself to speak, is biting.

'Don't assume Miss Pennyfields that the word privilege has any meaning for an innocent prisoner. Everything here is unwarranted punishment. You gave permission for me to work in a secluded place and I appreciated the consideration. Yes, I talked to Mary Burns. Thank god for a few minutes of civilized conversation with one intelligent inmate! I shall be glad to know her as a friend once we're both out of this hell hole. Goddam it! I can't believe that you of all people can be so petty!' She walks over to the door and stops, her back to the woman. 'Hah...and to think I was prepared to adore you for the rest of my born days!' She slams out of the room.


## Thursday afternoon 21st May

She's late for lunch and her rage persists as she eats her meagre portion. What a strict, heavy handed woman The Penny turns out to be. Why didn't she let her explain that Mary was deputising for an officer and she was just listening to her story? Did she think they were fucking? What a letdown! Daily contact with the "eff" word has insinuated it into her vocabulary. What the hell! If D. H. Lawrence used it to describe the sex act, so can she!'

News travels fast in prison. She's incensed by the new taunts but ignores them. "Asking for trouble Livesey, getting it off with Burns in the garden shed. Wait till Tracy hears about that." "You've spiked your Penny petard now Livesey." "Bad move 537."

Tracy and her gang must have eaten early, there's no sign of them. At one thirty Dee sets off for the laundry but the dining room "trusty" catches her before she's out of the door with the message that she must report to ROOM ONE.

The door of ROOM ONE bangs shut behind her and she knows immediately that this is it – this is the situation she was afraid might happen. ROOM ONE has been chosen for a battlefield and her opponents are lined up against her. A smirking Officer Morgan stands guard at the door, barring exit. Tracy, Bel and Rita face her and Bel has a knife. This is the flare-up she's been dreading. But she's ready, oh yes she's ready. She's fiercely bloody mad already. Little do they suspect!

She doesn't wait. She goes for Bel's eyes, both thumbs extended to sink into the sockets. Bel screams with pain and falls backward. Rita Dawson comes at her from the side. Dee swings her right arm with all her strength at Rita's face. There's a mighty crack and a violent pain in her arm. Then Tracy smashes a chair down on her forehead. She lunges to tear at Tracy's hair, misses but catches her finger in an earring as she's collapsing on to her knees. Tracy screams with pain.

Blood is pouring down Dee's face and her arm hurts so badly she thinks it must be damaged. She can't fight any more and closes her eyes. A vicious kick in her ribs makes her open them. She sees a uniform shoe before she keels over and loses consciousness. In between fainting spells she's aware of sirens and hurrying feet. The room is empty and quiet by the time two officers drag her to her feet and hand her a towel to hold to her head.

'She wants to see her,' Officer Morgan says. 'We'll take her up in the lift.' Dee is bundled unceremoniously through the governor's door. 'You sent for our not so innocent inmate,' Officer Morgan sneers before she goes out and bangs the door shut.

Dee sees The Penny tense and well she might! Her injured prisoner is furious and in a dreadful state. Why is she standing here in the governor's office when she needs medical attention? What good has it done, warning this woman that there might be trouble?

'You two faced bitch,' she hisses at The Penny. 'You sit up here in your ivory tower enforcing petty rules without a clue to what's happening downstairs. To think, I believed Frances when she said you would intervene when you knew what was going on. Taping that interview was a waste of breath and a betrayal of my confidence.'

The Penny jumps to her feet but her face wears a baffled expression.

'I hope you never forget this sight of me,' Dee carries on wildly, though she's having a job to stay upright. 'You're seeing an innocent woman, imprisoned by an interfering idiot of a detective, starved, humiliated, sexually abused and now beaten up. I've had no replies to the letters I've written. Were they sent? It must be against all the rules of human rights to let a prisoner be treated like this.' She needs to sit down and heads in the direction of the wing armchair but her legs give way. When she comes round, her head is resting on a pillow and she's covered with a blanket. She feels too ill to open her eyes. The Penny is making a phone call. 'Did you record the interview Frances?'.... 'Where did you leave the tape?'.... 'Elvira Morgan!'.... 'No, I wasn't on duty till this morning.'

Officer Waering arrives.

'Good God! Whatever's been going on?'

'Yvonne, take these keys,' The Penny says. 'Look in Joan's office for a cassette tape labelled *Prisoner 537 Livesey, Tuesday May 19th*. Frances Pointon left it on Joan's desk on Tuesday afternoon. If the tape isn't there, search every inch of property used by Elvira.'

'Good Lord!' Officer Waering utters her surprise and then the door closes.

Dee stirs. The pain makes her whimper. The Penny kneels beside her.

'An ambulance is on its way Mrs Livesey. I never received the tape Frances Pointon left for me. Can you tell me what happened this afternoon?'

Yes, she can, slowly and awkwardly. She describes the details of the fight.

'I'd been expecting trouble from those women. My attack was premeditated. I taught in a care-facility years' ago and was advised by the most frightening pupil I ever met, that if I was in trouble, I should go for the eyes. Ugh! Won't look very good on my rap sheet will it? Your laundry will have to do without me Miss Pennyfields. I'm out of it.' She drifts off into unconsciousness.

A loud knock on the door brings her round. She hears Officer Waering say, 'They were in Elvira's locker, the tape and letters, hidden underneath a towel.'

'That's what I suspected. I'm going to need a deputy Yvonne. Can you cope with the temporary position until the job can be advertised?' The Penny asks.

'Is it definite that she'll have to be sacked?'

'No doubt about it.'

'I'll talk it over with Gordon tonight.'

There's another knock on the door. This time it's the ambulance crew.

'Haven't we been having fun here today?' – a cheery voice says to Dee as she's being lifted on to a wheelchair and wrapped in blankets. 'This rumpus is keeping them busy at the hospital end.'

'You'll be okay Capability Brown,' Officer Waering teases.

'Say, "Hi," to Mary for me,' Dee whispers.

'I will, – see you in the prison infirmary next week.'

Dee knows Officer Waering is saying that to encourage her, but those farewell words are not what she needs to hear.


Thursday evening 21st May

Dee's arrival at Casualty is conspicuous for its lack of warmth. The nurses have already attended to Bel, Rita and Tracy before Dee is wheeled into a cubicle – they've assumed the worst. Dee hears the gossip.

'She's the one that killed her mother-in-law. Did you see it in the papers?'

'She must be an absolute fiend! Look what she's done to those other three prisoners.'

The last straw is Doctor Tupman sweeping into the cubicle in her usual manner. Dee shuts her eyes and keeps them closed. The desire for nil rapport is mutual. Doctor Tupman seems content to examine her injuries without an exchange of words. Dee flinches with pain a number of times and gives the doctor a clear indication as to where she's hurt. She hears the nurses speak to the doctor with respect. Doctor Tupman must have a good reputation. She certainly takes pains with stitching up the wound on her forehead.

Dee is shunted to the X Ray Department, to the plaster room, back to Casualty and, when her treatment is finished, to a side ward upstairs where two police officers are posted to keep her under close guard. A cup of tea and painkillers thankfully send her off into oblivion.

It's getting dark when voices disturb her. A nurse comes in to do the *obs*. The door opens a second time and Doctor Tupman is there, checking her chart. Dee feigns sleep. The Sister pops her head round the door and says quietly, 'There's a Miss Pennyfields to see you.'

'I should think so,' Doctor Tupman mutters, 'ask her to come in here please.' The police women leave the room.

There's a silence. Dee assumes that the two of them are examining her. They move away from the bed.

'Well, Madam Governor,' the doctor says in a loud whisper,' come to see the casualties from the battle at your establishment? I think you should make more effort to keep your inmates in order. You create a hell of a lot of work for us poor staff. I take it you've come to apologise?'

'Shouldn't we go outside Dot?' The Penny whispers.

'If I put my nose outside this door, someone will want me and it's nearly time for me to go off duty. We're okay here. You've got a desperate character in this one, haven't you? She hasn't spoken a word and we had to pull her about a bit.'

They carry on their conversation in loud whispers.

'She's not a desperate character.'

'Come on, Jane! An eye prodder, jaw breaker and ear ripper, not including the practice she's had with her mother-in-law?'

'Sh!'

'Why? What?'

'She didn't kill her mother-in-law as far as I can make out.'

'Oh my God!'

'I'm pretty sure she's innocent, shouldn't be in prison. The poor woman will have to serve the three months' remand sentence until she can be cleared – though I must add, she's not a poor woman when she's in a temper. She gave me what for this morning!'

'Why what had you done?'

'I came down on her like a ton of bricks for a minor breach of behaviour.'

'That's not like you. Did she get under your skin?'

'That's one way of putting it.'

'Oh my God Jane, we've all treated her like shit! Can't you do anything to get her out?'

'I've no evidence. I knew she wouldn't have an easy time of it in Stonebridge. She's educated, speaks differently. I assigned her to outside work that separated her from the other prisoners during the daytime. You know that patch of ground in front of the prison? She's got it looking like a garden already. I discovered today that my Deputy turned against her and ganged up with her cellmate and friends. She hid the tape that Frances recorded, the tape that would have let me know that they've had it in for her since the minute she arrived. I listened to the tape this afternoon after the hullabaloo had died down – some nice flattering comments about me.' Dee can tell that they're both amused. 'There was also information about the bullying. Did you think she looked thin?'

'She certainly hasn't been eating a lot lately and judging from the bruising on her ribs, she's had a mighty blow. She also has a cracked bone in her arm and the cut on her forehead.'

'I thought she looked badly hurt. Elvira Morgan kicked her when she was down, she saw the uniform shoe. Her roommate, Tracy Manners, the one with the ripped ear lobe, gave orders for her to be on starvation rations.'

'Why didn't she tell?'

'It's not that easy for prisoners to know who to trust, or how to get to me without officers and prisoners knowing what's going on. The tape was supposed to alert me.'

'You thought highly of Elvira Morgan didn't you?'

'Yes I did. I think she was jealous. She's had me on a pedestal, seemed to feel it was her duty to warn off anyone that came near me. She dislikes anyone I favour. Now I find out that she was also having an affair with Tracy Manners.'

'Cripes! I don't envy you your job. I haven't seen you for ages. What's the latest with the Monica affair?'

'Hmph!'

'I keep my ear to the ground. By all accounts, our handsome Renal Sister likes a finger in a lot of pies. I'm sorry I let you in for that.'

'It was my choice. She's an attractive madam. Do you fancy a drink? We could pop into The George. Barry and Jim are usually there about now.'

'Good idea. I'll ring Mark and get him to join us. He's been at Birmingham today, giving a paper.'

They leave and the police officers return. Dee asks for a drink and a nurse brings a milky bedtime drink, and two biscuits.

So – The Penny believes that she's innocent. Barren comfort considering the shocking state she's in, with ten more weeks of a remand sentence to serve. And The Penny and the doctor are friends – Barry, Jim and Monica? Who are they? Is The Penny a lesbian?

Dee wonders how Bel and Rita fare and which ward they're in. They wouldn't be expecting to come off worst this afternoon. And Tracy, she really asked for it. Perhaps she'll examine her temper a bit more seriously now that she's suffering. She won't be wearing an earring in that ear for a while.

And the fight, – she was ready to snap this afternoon. Her patience had worn thin. She got rid of a store of resentment at one fell swoop. It was one thing to lie in bed imagining a fight, as she'd done many times in the past when she was angry, it was quite another to hit out with intent to injure. It was horrible. What difference was there between her and a wild animal? What would Thea and Maddy have thought of their mother if they'd seen her lashing out?

She's demeaned herself. Tears well up and spill on to the pillow. She's allowed herself to enjoy sex with a woman. She's behaved in a silly flirtatious manner with Governor Pennyfields and then been rude to her. She's been too open in the interview with Frances Pointon. Where is the person she used to be? She's lost. She hurts all over and can't cope with the situation any longer. She lets go into despair, sobbing and wailing, past caring what anyone thinks. One of the officers leaves the room and returns with a doctor and a nurse.

'Mrs Livesey,' the doctor says, 'we can't have you distressing yourself like this. Nurse will administer a sedative.' The sedative is administered and puts paid to an eventful Thursday.

# WEEK THREE

Friday morning 22nd May

Dee is ready for the cup of tea that arrives on her bedside locker on Friday morning. She's not sure how she's supposed to reach it and grumbles as she twists her injured ribs to a sitting position.

'These may be qualified nurses but they're lacking in hands on care,' she says aloud.

'I'll get it nearer to you Mrs Livesey.' One of the police officers manoeuvres the locker to within reach.

Breakfast tastes good and is served in pleasing proportions. It's difficult for Dee to negotiate the food from the plate to her mouth with her left hand, but hunger prevails. After breakfast she lies back, not that injured ribs permit her to lie comfortably. At least her legs function well and she can get herself to the bathroom. At nine o'clock nurses rush in with clean bed linen.

'Bloody Tupman,' one of them snaps. 'Why can't she stick to the time for her usual round, same as the other doctors?' To Dee she says, 'Up.'

Her hospital gown is replaced with a clean one and she sits in an armchair while the bed is made. After a whirlwind few minutes she's back in bed.

Doctor Tupman reads her notes. 'More comfortable this morning?' she asks.

'Marginally, thank you,' Dee answers. She's far from comfortable and she's not going to say otherwise. She's concerned about the other prisoners. 'Could you tell me how the other Stonebridge patients are this morning please?'

The doctor gives her a long considered look. Dee knows that doctors don't usually pass on information about their patients but this doctor must think Dee needs to know because she says,

'One returned to Stonebridge, two going the same way today, all recovering.'

'Do you think my family will have been told that I'm in hospital?'

'That I can't say.'

'Who would be responsible for contacting them?'

'I'll make enquiries.'

'Thank you. I was allowed to phone them from the prison but I'm not sure what happens now. I'm still on remand.'

'Someone will get a message to you. I'll pop in again later.'

The message is brought by the Ward Sister. Dee's family has been informed that she's in hospital and that she's making a good recovery. Visiting is not permitted and it's not advisable for her to phone home in case there's a repeat of last night's distress.


## Saturday afternoon 23rd May

Dee sits out on the armchair after lunch. She hears the press of chattering visitors at the end of the corridor and slowly eases herself back on to the bed. She spreads the cellular blanket over her legs and dozes off. The scrape of a chair wakes her and who should be there but Frances Pointon!

'Frances!' she can't speak for crying; it's such a relief to see someone she knows and likes. 'I'll be all right in a minute,' she tries to assure her.

'Imagined you'd never see me again did you?' Frances teases. 'Oh dear, poor you... Listen Dee, I've got a friend with me, do you mind if she comes in?' Dee shakes her head.

A tall gracious woman takes her hand and holds it in a firm grip. There's something rather familiar about her attractive face and curly grey hair. Her clothes are expensive, classic summer-wear – but Dee has no recollection of seeing her before.

'Hello Dee, I'm Margaret Taylor,' the woman says. 'I'm glad you don't mind me accompanying Frances. She told me you'd come straight here from prison and we thought of a number of things you might need.' She unloads fruit, biscuits, a box of tissues and magazines from a capacious shopping basket. There's a pretty toilet bag and the article she missed this morning, a face flannel. 'I've brought some of my daughter's nightwear, would you care to try it for size.'

'Won't she mind?'

Margaret smiles sadly. 'My daughter Julia died three years ago Dee. It's time I parted with the nighties and this.' She unrolls a parcel wrapped in tissue paper and Dee looks in amazement at a beautiful silk kimono, pale blue and decorated with flowering pink cherry-trees. 'My husband's job took him abroad and this was one of his presents for Julia from Japan. Put it on. I'll help you. Once upon a very long time ago, I trained as a nurse.'

'Why are you giving these things to me?' Dee asks in bewilderment as the wide sleeves slip easily over her injured arm. 'You don't know me and surely there's someone in your family who would love them.'

'You're the only person I know who needs a nighty and dressing gown this afternoon,' Margaret says decidedly.

'Thank you so much! Never in my wildest dreams would I have imagined I'd own a silk kimono from Japan! I'll treasure it.'

'I'll be satisfied if you wear it.'

In the beautiful kimono, Dee leans back against the pillows and feels a much more respectable patient. But her mind is troubled. She needs to talk with Frances.

'Do you mind if I have a word with Frances,' she asks Margaret.

'Would you like me to leave?'

'No, no, I don't mind you listening,' – but she can't talk because she's choked with tears. Frances holds her hand and the contact steadies her. 'Frances, it was terrible yesterday,' she sobs and then tries to smile. 'The morning started okay because Mary Burns was required to act as a "trusty." She came to escort me to my work in the garden. Do you know her?'

'Yes.'

'I told you she's the only prisoner who's been kind to me. I wanted to hear why Mary is in prison. She said it made her cry to talk about it so we went into the potting shed and sat on the floor. Miss Pennyfields must have been watching. She sent for me and tore me off a strip! I never got a chance to explain that Mary was acting as a "trusty" because Officer Waering was held up in traffic. I was summarily relieved of the garden job. I was furious. I told her she was a petty woman and stormed out of her office.

'By lunchtime I was a seething mess and, when I was ordered to ROOM ONE and saw that I was cornered by the prisoners who don't like me, I blew. I did the attacking. I told you I was preparing for trouble but I hoped I'd never have to fight. I feel as though I'll never be the same again Frances, as though I've let myself down. I don't know how badly the prisoners meant to harm me. They might just have been trying to scare me. I was the savage one.'

'Weren't you reacting instinctively to protect yourself? What's the use of having instincts if we don't use them when it's necessary?'

'But I'd thought beforehand what I would do if anyone tried to harm me. I was in a rage.'

'Don't forget that I know some of the prisoners. I'm sure you've suffered more than enough provocation. Advance preparation was wise; you'll always know that you can behave savagely if a situation demands it. Your daughters have a mother tonight. There could have been a less fortunate end to your story.'

Doctor Tupman arrives at that point. She's greeted with pleasure by Dee's visitors. They all know each other!

'I'm afraid I've been very remiss as a doctor with regard to this patient,' Doctor Tupman confesses. 'It's given me a jolt.'

'You didn't default on your treatment,' Dee interrupts. 'You took great care with my head wound. It's just that you thought I was a killer. Come to think of it, I'd have been afraid of me yesterday.'

'Whether you were a killer or not, it was unethical to pre-judge you.'

'Well, perhaps you will think of prisoners more as persons in future.'

Doctor Tupman acknowledges the reprimand and nods in agreement. She disappears and when she returns, an orderly follows with cups of tea. They eat the home-made shortbread biscuits.

'How long will Dee have to stay in hospital?' Frances asks.

'Not long. She has injuries that can be supervised in a prison infirmary. I've asked for another x ray of her head, first thing on Monday morning. If it shows everything to be satisfactory, we wait for HMP headquarters to give us the all clear. Dee will be returned to Stonebridge. There's a possibility that, because she's had trouble there, she may be transferred to another prison'.

The joy goes out of the afternoon when Dee hears that. She doesn't deserve to be in prison. She hasn't committed a crime. There are ten more weeks left to be away from Thea and Maddy and she's already suffered enough.

'I don't think I can be cheerful anymore,' she says brokenly. 'Go now, please go. Thank you for being kind to me.' She bursts into uncontrollable crying.

Doctor Tupman summons the Sister and Dee is given sedatives. She sleeps for the rest of Saturday and most of Sunday.

## Monday morning 25th May

Dee dreads the arrival of Monday morning and wakes early enough to watch the sunrise. She's enjoyed the view of distant trees and doesn't want to exchange it for prison walls. Her desolation increases with every thought of returning to Stonebridge or being transferred to another prison. She gives way to more than one bout of hysterical crying. There aren't many tissues left in the box. She's not sure if she can hold on to the tatters of her former self, or even whether there's any point in trying. She's classed as a cargo of misdemeanour to be shipped wherever Her Majesty chooses. She's been tipped out of bed and it's ready made up for her return from the X Ray Department, or for the next unfortunate occupant. She sits on the armchair, wearing the silk kimono, ready for dispatch.

At half past eight she overhears the Sister say, 'She's here in this side ward.' She ushers in a tall bearded man with an identification tag on his suit jacket that reads HMP DR J BARRY. Dee's heart sinks.

'Deanna Livesey?' he says, reading the name on his clipboard.

'Yes.' She's not inclined to be helpful.

'Very good.' He reaches for her chart and studies it. 'I'm afraid I have to ask you some questions Deanna. The prison service is anxious to know how soon you can be returned to custody. Thank you Sister,' he says to the Sister and she leaves the room with a look of relief on her face – as do the two police officers. Dee notices that the door is left slightly open. 'Now, let me make a note of these details.' He scribbles on the pad and whispers urgently, 'We're getting you out of here. Don't look surprised.'

Surprised! What's going on? Who is this man? What does he mean by "we"? Dee is alarmed but hesitates to call out to the police officers. Before she can make her shocked mind decide to do anything, he says in his deep masculine voice, so that the listeners can hear, 'I see that you were admitted last Thursday, that makes this your fourth day.' He scribbles again and whispers, 'I'm a friend of Frances and Margaret, keep calm.'

She makes an effort to do as he says but she doubts if anyone watching would be convinced. Her eyes are wide with astonishment. 'This is crazy!' she whispers.

'You don't have to tell me! It was the only way to stop Margaret from doing something foolish.'

'Margaret Taylor?'

He nods and raises his voice. 'Now, this head wound…are you having headaches?'

'Yes, my head is painful all the time.'

'I see.' He whispers, 'Ever fainted?'

It's Dee's turn to nod.

Out loud he says, 'No other problems?'

'No apart from the fact that I hurt in lots of places.'

He whispers again, 'After the x ray.' He winks and gestures with a "thumbs up" that she's doing okay.

'Sister,' he calls and she comes back into the room. 'This head wound. Deanna complains that her head is painful but you and I know that headaches are normal after an injury of this kind.' She simpers at the compliment paid by the handsome doctor. 'Have the necessary checks been made?'

The Sister looks at her watch. 'Mrs Livesey is due to go down to the X Ray Department at nine o'clock.'

'Well Sister, if the x ray results indicate that there are no problems, I can safely say we'll have this patient back where she belongs before lunchtime. No need for your busy staff to be troubled by her any longer than necessary.' He checks his watch. 'Eight forty-five, we could make our way. The X Ray Department is on Ground Floor level?'

'Yes, a nurse will take you down.'

'We need a wheelchair.'

'Yes, Nurse!' A nurse is dispatched to bring a wheelchair.

'Deanna had better take her possessions with her. Prison transport will be ordered immediately if she's pronounced fit to leave.'

Their little procession causes quite a stir on the corridors. Dee is clutching a plastic bag that carries the contents of her locker. She's surprised that the banging of her heart doesn't make the bag rustle! One policewoman is handcuffed to her wrist. The nurse pushes the wheel chair and the doctor and second policewoman walk alongside. Staff and patients draw to one side to let them pass and everyone stands clear of the lift doors.

When they arrive at the  Ray Department, the patients already waiting on the rows of chairs see the handcuffs and move nervously. Dee is just a specimen of compliant baggage. She's glad none of them can see or hear her heart pounding.

'Nurse, you could go back to the Ward,' Doctor Barry says. 'The officers and I will see Deanna safely in for her x ray. We'll get a message up to the ward if she has to stay in hospital for a few more days. I think it's more likely that we'll be phoning for prison transport.'

The nurse leaves. It's Dee's turn to enter the cubicle. The radiographer is holding her appointment papers. Her eyes are frightened; she's made the connection between Dee's name and her reputation. She looks at Doctor Barry.

'It'll be all right. I'll come in with her,' he says reassuringly.

'The two police officers will have to wait outside,' the radiographer says. 'If she can walk, leave the wheelchair outside.'

The handcuff attaching her to the Police Officer is unlocked. Doctor Barry takes the carrier bag and holds Dee's arm as they walk into the room. He retires behind the protective screen. Dee slides herself slowly and painfully on to the hard bed and turns into different positions as directed.

'Right, she can get up now. We'll have these processed,' the radiographer says.

Dee raises herself slowly and pauses on the edge of the bed. Pain and dizziness combined, it's not too difficult to imagine the peculiar head sensation before a faint. She puts her feet to the floor and slithers down onto the cold linoleum.

Doctor Barry kneels down beside her. 'Deanna! Deanna Livesey! She's out cold,' he says to the radiographer 'It may be a genuine faint but we can't be too sure. If it's a faint she'll be round in a minute.'

'Shall we get the policewomen in?'

'I've a better idea. Can I use your phone? Does that door open?' Dee hears him dial. 'Officer Graham? Problem in the X Ray Department. Prisoner Livesey has collapsed, probably a faint. We can't take any chances, she may be faking. Bring the prison transport vehicle round to, where shall I say?' he asks the trembling radiographer.

'On to the road by the car-park reserved for the medical staff.'

'Doctors' car-park, – be ready with the cuffs when you see an open door.'

Dee stirs.

'Deanna? Deanna Livesey? Can you pull yourself together now? Let's have you on your feet.'

Her effort to stand is convincingly painful and awkward. She's only one arm that works properly, her ribs hurt like mad and her head is woozy after the few minutes flat down on the floor. She feels the fresh air and knows that the door is open. She leans back against the bed. They all hear the sound of running footsteps. A male and female prison officer push the door open wide. The male officer gets behind Dee and grabs her arms.

'No, no,' she screams, 'my arm!'

'Officer Rigby,' the man barks and the female officer steps forward. Dee's good arm is seized and she's handcuffed to Officer Rigby. She's led out toward a parked van with its rear doors open.

'Let the policewomen know what has happened please,' Doctor Barry says from the doorway. 'They'll be able to return to their local station. Thank you for your cooperation. You will see that the x rays are forwarded to the hospital at Stonebridge?'

By that time, Dee is too far away to hear the reply. Doctor Barry gets into the passenger seat and the van pulls away.

There doesn't appear to be any haste but, once out of the hospital grounds, the van very soon turns off the main road into side roads. It stops where large windowless factory walls line both sides of the street. Her handcuffs have been unlocked on the way. Now the doors are opened and Doctor Barry says, 'Out as quick as you can.'

A sea-green Cortina is parked facing in the opposite direction. He and Dee bundle into the back seat and the car zooms off, cuts down a side road and zigzags for two miles through streets of terraced houses, until they turn into the tree shaded road that borders Lineham Park. A number of vehicles are parked in the road but the Cortina is able to draw up in a convenient space behind a grey Morris Oxford. The driver's door opens and a tall, fair man in a white shirt, grey flannels and with a baseball cap cheekily back to front on his head, strolls over to them. He shakes hands with the doctor and they make a play of greeting Dee like one of the family. The fair man helps her into the passenger seat of the Morris Oxford, waves cheerio to the others and seats himself in the driver's seat. He switches on the engine.

'Deanna Livesey?' he says urgently and she nods. 'I thought I'd better check before I whisk you away.' They drive off. 'I didn't really need to ask,' he says. 'I doubt there's another kimono in town like Julia's. Let's get clear of the city before they have time to mount any road blocks.'

Julia! How does this man know Julia?

He heads south of the city, negotiates traffic lights and roundabouts and glances incessantly into the mirrors. Dee can tell that he's worried about pursuit. The little thrill of hope and excitement that shivers through her is quickly erased by anxiety. She's an accessory to evading a prison sentence. What a risk these strangers are taking on her behalf. Why are they doing it? Can it work? Will she be able to see her children? Five miles further on they turn onto a garage forecourt and drive round the back to where a smart red sports car is parked. Dee is transferred to the sports car. A fistful of notes is thrust into the garage owner's hand.

'Geoff, valet the Morris straight away please, starting with the passenger side?' He stays to watch the mechanic begin the work. 'Neat?' he says to Dee once they set off. 'No one will suspect that my Opel GT, with its smart green stripes on the bonnet, is transporting an escaped prisoner. Okay! You deserve an explanation. I'm Barry Pennyfields, brother to my impressive prison governor sister Jane.' Dee sits in the car seat, a crumpled heap of shock and surprise, scarcely believing her ears. 'If you're wondering why we've kidnapped you I suppose it started as Jane's fault and then mother jumped on to your case. Jane came home in a pretty weird state after you'd been admitted to Stonebridge.'

'How do you mean 'weird'?'

'Well, not her usual self. I was actually quite worried about her. I was playing some slow jazz records when she got home. Mum was in the kitchen putting finishing touches to the meal and Jane and I danced to Louis Armstrong's latest song, *We have all the time in the world*. The song seemed to cut her up. She cried, made a wet patch on my shirt. Mum came to say the meal was on the table and saw Jane's tears. That was enough to ruffle her mother-hen feathers. We don't all get together often you see, and Mum loves it when we do. She goes to town with the meal and we drink wine and sit and natter all evening. That Friday, after you appeared on the prison scene, Jane didn't seem as though her thoughts were with us. We'd all read about the woman who pushed her mother-in-law out of the bedroom window,' he said, glancing sideways at her and laughing at her grimace. 'Jane suddenly asked Frances if she was due to visit the prison the following Tuesday. '

'Frances! Frances Pointon? She was at your family meal! Is she a relative?'

'Ah...another story, tell you some time. Of course, Frances wanted to know why Jane was asking and that's when Jane said you were not guilty of murdering your mother-in-law.' Dee shudders every time the murder is referred to. 'Sorry Dee, tactless of me. Anyway, Jane went up to her flat after the meal, didn't even have coffee,'

'Was that unusual?'

'I'll say so. She's got her own kitchen in her flat. She can make a drink up there but she always goes through to the drawing room with us for coffee after dinner. She likes to look at Mum's sewing and craft magazines. Mum's a wow at embroidery and patchwork and stuff. Jane disappeared upstairs and played pop music all night.'

'That's a good way to relax. I wait till my husband goes out and then I play pop music and dance.'

'But Jane's a classical music buff.'

'So am I, but popular songs help you to wind down.'

'You may be right. She's not long been out of a love affair, she may have needed to mooch a bit.'

That did interest Dee but it was not her place to follow up with an enquiry.

'Or she could have been tired,' she tried to think herself into The Penny's shoes. 'It must be a heck of a job being in charge of the prison.'

'Mm…could be. I know she worries if she's convinced that someone's innocent. You see she can't get anyone out. They have to wait for the judicial wheels to turn. She does her best. She told us she'd given you the gardening job to keep you away from the other prisoners in the daytime and roped Mum and me into helping. I'm keen on roses and Mum on perennials.'

'That answers a question for me. I wondered who had handwritten the labels on the plants that arrived.'

'Oh yes, that was Mum. Mum asked Frances to weigh you up; she's a fierce hen when any of her brood is disturbed. She's lost Julia and partly blames herself for encouraging Julia to be a fashion model. I suppose that her alarm bells rang when Jane behaved out of character. Daft isn't it, when you think that Jane is in charge of a prison.'

'Just a minute Barry, Julia's mum is Margaret.'

'Yes, that's right and she's my mum and Jane's.'

'She said her name was Margaret Taylor!'

'Oh yes, I forgot. She used her maiden name. The whole kidnap thing was her idea. She's a wonderful mother but headstrong. If she gets an idea in her head she can't be trusted to behave sensibly. She was determined to get you out and we thought it would be safer if we did the job ourselves, planned and executed the escape I mean. God knows what would have happened if she'd tried it herself. What would you have thought, Dee? She suddenly calls on Jim and me on Saturday afternoon and asks us to kidnap you from hospital – and it has to be done on Monday, today, because otherwise you might be transferred to another prison! We could understand that the state you were in had triggered Mum's grief about Julia, but it took some swallowing to realise that she was determined to go ahead with rescuing you.'

Dee is stunned. 'Jane mustn't find out we're behind the kidnap or we'll all end up inside. It was my partner Jim who got you out.'

'Doctor Barry?'

He grins. 'Clever wasn't it? He's an ambulance driver and knows the hospital layout. He knew about the extra door out of the X Ray Department because he sometimes has to use that entrance to take a patient in on a stretcher.

'His first choice of career was the church but the attitude to homosexuality made him withdraw from the training. He says that as long as he's helping people in some capacity or other that will do for him. I'm the same really. Dad wanted me to, "do something" with my fine art degree but I decided to be a hairdresser. My work makes people feel good. I think Dad was disappointed. He was a clever lawyer bod, but this career suits me. I have a hairdressing salon and I do make-up for the amateur dramatic society. I'm good at disguises. When you see Jim's normal appearance you'll see the brilliance of my efforts.'

'I notice modesty's not your strong point.'

He laughs. 'Never has been.'

Dee has also noted the comment about homosexuality. Being rejected by the church – that fits in with what she's heard. Yet Barry is so nice and friendly. How could anyone reject Barry? She hasn't really met Jim. She was impressed with his deep voice and strong physique and the way he handled the pretend emergency. He and Barry are opposites, Jim dark and sturdy, Barry slim and fair. She can't find it in herself to object to the fact that they live together and have sex – how could she after her Tracy Manners experience?

'Barry, what motivated your mother to suggest a kidnap?'

'Ah…one or two whys and wherefores I gather, though who knows how Mum's mind works? She suffered terribly when Julia died. When Jane mentioned that you were innocent, she was upset at the unnecessary separation from your daughters. On Saturday she suspected that you were near breakdown and was convinced that you had to be got out. We argued like mad because we were shit-scared of the idea. We tried to get it into her that there are loads of suffering prisoners and one can't go round helping them all, but she'd got the bee in her bonnet and here we are.'

Dee's mind is full of disturbed thoughts. She looks out at the scenery. This is her favourite time of the year for hedgerows. The cow parsley is tall and feathery. The overhanging sprays of white hawthorn blossom cast shadows on the road but they, and the bluebells she spies amongst the trees, are past their best. Already the meadows are growing yellow with buttercups.

'Where are we going?'

'To Hattersley House, our home. You won't be able to stay there because Jane's due home for the weekend on Friday. I'm arranging transport with a long distance van driver for your removal to a safe place, probably on Friday morning. Mum wants you to have a few days to rest and recover before you leave.'

'What about tracing the escape-vehicles?'

'The car is Pete's. He took charge of all that. He's a crazy coot, loves dare-devil schemes. His friend did a skilled job on both sets of number plates, made them out of ply wood. They'll be burnt by now.'

'And the van?'

'It is a black delivery van. I hope it wasn't around long enough for anyone to realise that it wasn't official prison transport. Both vehicles will have been valeted by now. I don't think you touched any door handles did you? Anyway, they'll all have been wiped clean. Connor and his wife Ann played their parts credibly as prison officers didn't they? It's been quite a rush to get the uniforms and all the details sorted since Saturday.'

Dee's chin wobbles, – these kind people taking dangerous risks for her. She fishes in her dressing gown pocket for a tissue.

'Don't worry Dee,' Barry says gently, 'it was scary but it's done now.'


## Hattersley House

This part of the country road is familiar. They drive under a bridge that carries the main London railway line and take a lane that turns left, up a hill. Dee recognises the house. It's a large yellow sandstone mansion with a walled garden, stables and outhouses. She always looks out for it from the train. Her stomach does a flip-flop when they turn in at the gates. Barry scrunches the car to a stop on the gravel in front of the portico and helps her up the steps. Margaret is waiting and there, inside the door, is one large expanse of Minton tiled hall floor. The Penny was not exaggerating.

The kitchen is painted cream and is large and airy. Margaret brings the kettle to the boil on the Aga hotplate and fills a Brown Betty teapot. There are freshly baked shortbread biscuits cooling on a wire tray, looking very similar to the ones they ate in hospital. It's warm and delightful, a wonderful relief to be away from the hospital and prison. Here are people whom she doesn't know and they're making her welcome, whereas all she can do is worry about the consequences.

'I don't mean to put a damper on your plans,' she says apprehensively, 'but what if The Penny comes home unexpectedly?'

'Jane lives at her flat in town during work periods; she would let Mum know in advance if she was coming.' In her nervous state Dee is not comforted by Barry's assurance. 'By the way Mum, where's Frances?'

'She couldn't stand me wittering about everything and went off to call on Mrs Green. Mr Green's our gardener,' Margaret explains.

'Does Frances live here?'

'When Frances retired from the Probation Service, Dee, she agreed to come here as housekeeper. My husband Hugh was an invalid and it was all too much for me. You can see that this place needs a lot of keeping up, even though it has been divided into flats. Jane and Barry are responsible for looking after their apartments. When Hugh died two years ago, Frances offered to return to her own home but...'

'Come on Mum! I said I'd tell you later didn't I Dee? To all intents and purposes Frances...'

'Barry!'

He laughs loudly. Dee gets the impression that he's an irrepressible character.

'Okay Mum, I'll tell it right.'

Margaret intervenes. 'The truth is...that I asked her to stay on because I liked her company.'

'More like a half-truth!' her son quibbles.

'Oh, dear Dee, – the long story is that I've known Frances since her first day at Grammar School. I met her on a corridor looking panic stricken because she'd got separated from her class and was lost. She was ready to run off home. I came across her when I was waltzing back gaily to my classroom, after an inspection with the nit nurse.'

'And Frances has loved her from that day to this!' Barry sings out.

'Yes, well, something of the sort. I wasn't aware that Frances was in love with me Dee. I found that out from Jane. Frances and Jane meet for lunch in town on prison-visiting days. That's when Frances told Jane about her feelings. She said she was too uncomfortable to continue to live close to me, when there were just the two of us in the house. Jane knew I didn't want her to leave Hattersley, so my professional daughter gave me a talking to. She's experienced in dealing with women and their relationships.'

'In other words Mother dear, Jane helped you to realise how much you care for Frances and now you both live together, happily ever after.' Barry hugs his mum and pours a second cup of tea.

'I hope you can cope with our household Dee,' Margaret says anxiously. 'The percentage of same sex relationships is higher than usual in our family.'

Margaret is a loveable woman, so easy to be with. Dee likes her openness. There are so few friends with whom she can be entirely herself; she has to be careful not to embarrass one or other of them. She feels that she can confide in Margaret.

'I'm afraid my head is in a muddle about relationships between women,' she confesses. 'Did Frances tell you about my roommate?'

'No, she's not allowed to go into details about her clients. She just said you were having a rough time.'

'My cellmate, Tracy Manners, is a lesbian. She insisted on having sex with me almost every night. I haven't thought myself outside my marriage, such as it is,' she says disconsolately. 'I come from a world where there's no discussion along these lines.'

'You'll get it sorted,' Barry asserts. 'Drink your tea. Biscuits taste good Mum.'

Dee finds it difficult to believe that she's being made welcome in a mansion, by people she's only just met. It's like a fairy tale, as though Margaret has waved a magic wand – but what will happen to them if the police track them down? What about The Penny's job if the connection is discovered? What about herself and her children? Has she unwittingly allowed herself to be inveigled into a worse situation? It's too dreadful at this stage to contemplate capture, re-imprisonment and punishment.

'I'm concerned about the consequences of your rescuing me,' she falters. 'It's a huge relief not to be transferred to another prison, I can't deny that. But the whole escape was like being caught up in a whirlwind. After the first alarm, when Jim said he was there to get me out, it didn't occur to me to put up any opposition. I went along with his idea of fainting. That makes me an accessory.'

'There wasn't an easy way to get you out,' Margaret said. 'If you'd been fit, you might have weathered the prison experience but when I saw your injuries on Saturday and your highly nervous state, I feared the worst for you and your girls. A complete nervous breakdown wouldn't help you or them.'

'It was a wild plan on your part Mum, don't make excuses,' Barry cut in. 'We pointed out to you that there must be thousands of prisoners in danger of collapse and no one is there to rescue them. God knows what would have happened if we'd let you attempt it yourself.'

'People get away with murder – it's in the paper every day!' Margaret said defensively. 'I've never broken the law. I've often wondered whether I'd have had the courage to fight alongside the suffragettes if I'd lived earlier this century.'

'Oh you would! I could see you chained to a railing and Dad using his influence to get you out of trouble. You didn't leave Jim and me any option other than to stop you from doing something crazy.'

'It was splendid of you both to take the matter out of my hands. Barry, I do know how fortunate I am to have a resourceful son with willing friends.'

'Never again Mum! I was scared stiff! We were up at the crack so that I could fix Jim's disguise. He looked great, didn't he Dee, utterly convincing as a doctor. But was I glad when the Cortina appeared! The poor sods who own black vans and sea-green Cortinas will be grilled by the police tonight. Pete seemed to be thoroughly enjoying the escapade. He might consider a kidnap to be fun but I feel as though my nerves will jangle for days.'

'If it helps you to calm down, I solemnly promise that there will be no repeat of today's adventure. It has taken its toll on my nerves and driven Frances out. Now Dee, let's get you upstairs for a bath and rest before lunch.'

'I'll blow-dry your mop when you've washed it,' Barry says, 'then I must get back to the salon. The establishment might founder without its proprietor.'

Margaret takes the greatest care of her in the bath, aware of her painful ribs, washing her hair gently and keeping the plaster on her arm dry. 'I like to get my hands on a patient,' she says. 'The children came along as soon as I was married. I never got chance to put my nurse's training into practice.'

'I'm sorry you have to go to all this trouble.'

'Put that idea out of your head Dee. This has worked a small wonder for Barry. He knows you'll sleep in the bed in Julia's flat. He hasn't set foot in her flat in the three years since she died. And here he is – promising to come up and do your hair.'

Barry arrives with brush and hair-dryer and speedily, so that Dee doesn't have to sit for long, he dresses her short hair-style. She feels beautifully clean and pretty, propped against a bank of pillows, in another of Julia's nighties and with a featherweight shawl over her shoulders.

'On Saturday your mum made me feel like a respectable prisoner, today I feel like a respectable escaped prisoner.'

'All part of the Pennyfields' service.' Barry waves the tools of his trade aloft in a gesture of farewell.

They hear a loud, 'Cooee' from downstairs.

'That's Frances,' Margaret says. 'I bet she's itching to know if the kidnap was successful. You have a rest Dee – I'll call you for lunch.'

The phone call from Stonebridge Women's prison comes just as they sit down for afternoon tea. Frances and Dee keep as still as mice. Margaret turns her back on them so that she can concentrate on the call and feign ignorance of the news.

'What a shock,' she gasps. 'Does that mean we were all deceived by the Livesey woman?'....

'I'm so sorry dear.' She manages to sound regretful. 'I thought she seemed quite nice. I can't believe that she was sitting in that hospital bed planning to escape.'....

'Well yes, you do know what these women are like but you did think Dee was a bit different didn't you?' She clutches her fist to her mouth. She said "Dee" not Livesey. Jane hasn't noticed.

'Don't let it upset you Jane. You've a prison full of women to keep you occupied and you did get that patch of garden tidied up.' ....

'Yes, you were lucky she didn't run. At least she didn't break your trust where the garden was concerned..' ....

'We're going to have afternoon tea now dear. Will you be able to get off home soon or has this escape meant more work for you?' ....

'Oh, I understand. What a nuisance. Well, you'll be here for dinner on Friday.' ....

'Not until Saturday?' ....

'Enjoy the concert. Who's playing?' ....

'Right, see you Saturday lunchtime. Look forward to it. Hope you don't have too difficult a time between now and then.'

She flops down on a chair. 'She's going to the Halle at The Victoria Hall on Friday night, with Annabel Priestley, the Vice-Principal of Deanswood. That gives us an extra day to plan and more time, Dee, for you to recover before your removal to base two. Sorry if we make you sound like a package. Frances, who's this Annabel Priestley? Has Jane spoken about her?'

'Yes, Deanswood is the Further Education College Jane told me about at lunch last Tuesday,' Frances says. 'Jane was booked to give a talk to the senior students and Annabel Priestley was in charge of the arrangements. It's also the reason why Jane wasn't there to receive the tape of your interview Dee. The fighting could have been avoided and you might have survived until July. Ah well...so Jane is going to a concert with Annabel Priestley. I believe Annabel is bi-lingual. Her mother's French, lives in Paris.

What next I wonder? I'll make the tea Margaret. You must be exhausted after that convincing bit of deception.'

## Tuesday 26th May

Margaret tiptoes into Dee's bedroom twice in the night to see if she's all right. She brews a pot of tea in Julia's kitchen at six o'clock and makes them each a slice of toast and marmalade. Dee asks her about Julia.

'I'll get the family photograph album,' Margaret says and goes through to Julia's living room. When she comes back she perches on the bed beside Dee.

'Julia followed thirteen months after Barry,' she explains, when Dee comments on the numerous toddler-stage photos of the two of them playing together. Jane is the serious little girl with fair bobbed hair and a fringe.

As the years pass, the photos of Julia tend to be pages cut from magazines, records of glamorous photo shoots abroad.

'I took Julia down to London to see the Festival of Britain in 1951. She fell in love with the world of fashion when she was still a teenager. Hugh and I helped her to get a flat in London, and Hugh kept an eye on her, whenever his work took him to town. She was very much in demand as a model and, as you can see from the photos, she was often abroad – on holiday if not on a photo shoot.

'I began to get phone calls rather than visits,' Margaret says sadly. 'One weekend Julia brought a man home that was a lot older than her. They seemed happy but I thought Julia looked thin and strained. I sneaked into her flat when they were out and searched everywhere. I found pills and wrote down the name. My doctor explained that if Julia was taking those pills she must be a serious drug user.

'She arrived home full of enthusiasm when Hugh and I decided to turn the house into flats and threw herself into choosing colours and furniture. She liked everything to be light and pretty, hence the white and gold in her living room, the white and pink in here.

'Jane's flat is like another world. She kept her father's oak desk, his brown leather couch and the rugs and lamps we brought back from our travels in Morocco and Turkey. Her living room has a warm, rich effect. It's very welcoming.'

'That sounds like her office at the prison.'

'Yes, Jane insists on a pleasant workplace.'

'What about Barry's flat?'

'His flat is upstairs. Fine, fine and delicate I would use to describe Barry's taste. Stainless steel, glass, exquisite fabrics, flower prints. I never go into Jane or Barry's flat unless invited but I spend a lot of time in here,' she says quietly.

'Julia kept her lovely appearance until she was nearly thirty but by then she was injecting herself and her eyes were hollow. I was terrified for her and pleaded with her to get help. 'I can't manage without it Mum,' she said hopelessly. 'She didn't stay that time, I think because she couldn't bear to see me worrying. I didn't see her again. We had a phone call.'

She turns to the back of the photo album. There's a photo of Julia's grave and on the headstone *Julia Pennyfields Died age 29*. It's dated 1967.

'She would have been my age,' Dee whispers.

Margaret closes the album and they sit in silence, holding hands.

The savoury smell of bacon creeps into the room.

'That's Frances' way of getting us moving,' Margaret says. She slides off the bed and carries the book of precious memories through to Julia's living room.

The three of them sit cosily in dressing gowns and Dee begins the first of four days at Hattersley with a delicious breakfast. Frances disappears behind her newspaper. Dee stares at the headlines, PRISONER ESCAPES. Underneath is a dreadful photo of her, taken a fortnight ago as she was leaving the courtroom. The article reports that the police are doing everything in their power to discover the whereabouts of Deanna Livesey.

'Fancy alerting the country to be afraid of me,' she says in a small voice, – 'and how awful for my family to see that photo and read that column. What will Thea and Maddy think if they see their mother looking so horrible? I was just beginning to hope that things might come right and now I'm appalled. Do good and bad things have to happen at the same time?'

'In my experience they do Dee,' Margaret says. 'There's always pain running alongside pleasure. It's called life.'

'Can you cut out that article and keep it for me please Frances? I hope it won't be long before I can paste it next to, PRISONER RELEASED, in my scrapbook.

# WEEK FOUR

Saturday 30th May

They're all restless even though Margaret assures them that Jane never arrives before lunchtime on a Saturday. The last call from van driver Greg informed them that he's past the accident spot on the M6 and traffic is moving freely. Barry calculates that he'll arrive in another three quarters of an hour. It's already ten fifty.

Dee is in a fearfully nervous state. Margaret has removed the bulky dressing from the wound on her forehead and replaced it with a flesh coloured plaster. Jane's wardrobe has been raided by her determined mother, a virago who disregards all niceties with regard to her daughter's privacy in order to complete the job in hand. Dee has to wear Jane's trousers with turn ups because Jane is the taller of the two of them. Her shirts fit Dee and a loose cardigan hides her fractured arm.

'Let's get Dee's luggage in the car Mum,' Barry says anxiously. 'What's all this,' he questions when he sees the large zipper bag and three carrier bags.

'This one has clothes for Dee and the other has food for the journey, for both of them.'

'You're a good un Mum.' He hugs her. 'You ready Dee?'

'Yes, I'm ready. Can we go now and wait somewhere for the van?

'We'll give it until eleven thirty and then set off. Here's Frances with coffee.'

'Don't be in such a hurry Dee.' Frances scolds. 'You didn't eat much breakfast. Come and have coffee and biscuits on the patio.'

They can't relax despite the beautiful morning and all breathe a sigh of relief when the minute-hand points to eleven twenty-five.

'Not that we want to part with you dear,' Margaret says, 'but I do have a fiercely professional daughter. You've given me the phone numbers I need. I'll find a way of letting your family know you're safe and in good hands. There's no need for you to worry about anything; concentrate on getting better in the coming weeks. Greg will bring you back to Hattersley at the end of July.'

Margaret reiterates everything she's said, more than once, in the last tense moments. Dee doesn't mind the repetition because the news that she's welcome to return to Hattersley is a comfort. Once she and her luggage are safely stowed in the car, Barry drives out of the gateway – narrowly avoiding the white Jaguar that turns into the drive.

'Whew! Damn! That was a near one. Wouldn't Jane come early just when we don't want her to? Now she'll want to know why I didn't stop, dammit!' Barry curses and puts his foot down.


## Sunday 31st May

Greg drives his van on to the station car-park at Thurso and draws up alongside a Jeep. He switches off the engine. The driver's door of the Jeep opens and a woman in tartan slacks and Barbour jacket, grey hair drawn into a chignon, jumps down and walks across to them. Her face is unsmiling as Greg helps a stiff and achy Dee out of the van. She needs his hand to steady her.

'Doctor Hunter?' Greg enquires.

She nods and they shake hands.

'Here's your visitor safe and sound Doctor Hunter. She's been grand company. I've never known a journey north pass so quickly. Well Dee, I must be off if I'm to catch the ferry – to Orkney,' he adds for Doctor Hunter's information. 'I can't hug you in your painful state Dee. It'll have to be a wee kiss. I'll see you here on Tuesday 28th July at eight o'clock. Cheerio for now.'

Doctor Hunter picks up Dee's bag before she can get to it.

'So you're called Dee,' she says shortly. 'Margaret said your name was Deanna Livesey. My name's Elspeth. I can't spend eight and a half weeks being called Doctor Hunter.'

Dee knows immediately that she's not welcome. Her spirits sink to their lowest ebb since she was wrenched from her home.

Greg took such good care of her on the journey. He'd made up a little bed in the back of the van with a lilo, a pillow and blankets. Once he braked sharply and Dee rolled against the shipment of pottery that was on its way up to his sister's B&B venture in Kirkwall. He called out to her anxiously. She groaned and laughed, said she was all right, and crawled back on to her makeshift bed.

Greg knew the route well and made sure that their stopping places would not draw attention to an escaped prisoner. The toilets were always accessible without going through a café or past other travellers and he was a reassuring presence waiting for her just outside. They were the same age so she supposed there was nothing unusual in seeing a driver take care of his woman passenger.

Dee knew they'd left Glasgow behind and taken the Loch Lomond route north but they were well past Fort William and driving along Loch Ness before she enquired about their destination.

'At last...I wondered when you were going to ask. I thought your prison experience had knocked all the curiosity out of you.'

'I do feel that for three weeks I've had no control over my life and I might just as well wait and see what happens next. On the other hand, if I'm to spend two months in a place, I suppose I'd better know where it is.'

'I'm to drop you off at Thurso. You're to be met there by a Doctor Hunter.'

'Mrs Pennyfields thought it advisable to keep all information from me, apart from saying that I was being sent to a doctor who has been her friend for years. She wouldn't name her.'

'Sensible woman, she couldn't have arranged for you to stay in a more distant spot. You've a thirty mile ride along the north coast when you leave Thurso.'

Dee travelled with Greg in the cab for some of the journey. She liked to see the roadside flowers, Ragged Robin and Stitchwort, Gorse bushes in bloom, towering larches and pines. In the evening they had to stop for a rest period. Greg stretched out on the cab seat and Dee had a nap on her makeshift bed.

It was eerie to drive through the night and see the looming shapes of hills in the dark. They both exclaimed with delight when dawn brought colour to the landscape.

Now, sitting by this unfriendly doctor she feels banished and unwanted. As soon as the Jeep halts she sees an attractively painted sign, *Hunters' Lodge,* and knows they've arrived. She opens the door and climbs down. The property stands by itself, overlooking a wide bay. No one is likely to trace her to this isolated residence. It's a large, single storey, double fronted stone cottage. There's a low stone wall round the garden and a gate, painted green, which leads to a pathway down to the beach.

'Will it be all right for me to go down to the beach for some fresh air? I'm stiff after so many hours sitting in a vehicle.'

Doctor Hunter nods and carries her luggage into the house.

Dee stands and breathes in the fresh salty air. From that raised position she can see right across the wide beach that curves away to the distant hillside. The wind blows the swathes of tough grass and they shimmer. What a splendid view. If only Thea and Maddy were here to share it with her, and her Mum. Her Scottish mum loves the Highlands.

She steps cautiously down the pebbly path to the sand, turns left and walks underneath the overhanging cliff, picking her way between the rocks. She chooses a smooth, fairly level surface and sits down, leaning wearily against the boulder that backs on to her seat. This could all be so beautiful in different circumstances. At least, her unhappy spirit can commune with this lonely scene.

She's been going over and over the seriousness of her situation since last Monday. Her immediate delight at the astonishing rescue from the hospital, which she felt was justified at first because she's innocent, soon vanished. She can't ignore the reality that she's a fugitive from the law.

In her physically abused and injured state, she was only too ready to let herself accept the comfort of good food, lovely surroundings and the Hattersley offer of unconditional care. Should she now give herself up and serve the rest of her sentence? Would it be a better option than staying here where she's not wanted? She would probably be kept in a prison hospital for five weeks until her arm was ready to come out of plaster. By then she would be feeling stronger and could cope with the other prisoners. Thea and Maddy could come on visiting days, if the distance to the prison wasn't too far to travel.

How can she contact the police from this remote place? Doctor Hunter might drive her to a public phone box. In no way must she implicate her, the Pennyfields' family or their associates. Would they be disappointed if she undid all their good efforts by giving herself up? Families didn't usually involve themselves in extraordinary schemes just because a beloved son or daughter died. Now she's away from them, she can see how delightfully eccentric Barry and Margaret are, and how easy and privileged their lifestyle. Their homosexuality would shock her mum and dad. It was a topic that was rarely mentioned in her home and it wasn't spoken of in a kindly manner by any of her acquaintances.

Perhaps it would be better to "turn herself in". It was all very well for people to help her but it undermined her integrity and responsibility for her own choices. On the other hand, it wasn't her fault that her life had been disrupted by a false accusation. Why should she care about obeying the law?

Her options don't seem very clear. It would certainly make Governor Pennyfields' position easier if she was back behind bars. Does that fact matter more than her own unfair situation? She wonders if Margaret explained Barry's hasty departure satisfactorily.

She sits on. She's weary. Perhaps it would be better to decide what to do when she's rested. A few days in this healthy region should bring the colour back to her cheeks. The seat's cold. The boulder's cold but both are preferable to the coldness of the attitude up in the cottage.

She knows she must move. She mustn't further irritate her hostess by being rude. Doctor Hunter is Margaret's friend and it's obliging of her to accommodate an escaped prisoner. She walks slowly back, brushing the sand off her clothes. She glimpses Doctor Hunter looking for her but she disappears quickly. Poor woman, does she think her charge has run away? Perhaps she hopes she's run away.

Dee realises she's hungry when the enticing smell of bacon and strong coffee greet her. Her hostess has cut up the sausages and bacon so that she can spear them with her fork. She's placed

Dee at the table facing the living room/studio. Dee is fascinated by the examples of the doctor's paintings and weaving in natural colours. They don't find anything to say to each other so Dee has time to study the work. One painting in particular, a wide seascape mounted on an easel, holds her attention. Dee feels she can relate to that representation of vastness.

'Do you like it?' Doctor Hunter asks suddenly.

'Oh yes,' she says and carries on chewing. 'But...'

It's audacious to criticize this woman's work but Dee is artistic and she has an opinion. Also there's the element of "don't care" because the woman doesn't like her anyway. She gets up from her seat and goes over to the picture. 'It needs, a tiny solitary figure, here. Back toward the viewer, hair and skirt blowing in the wind and then you can give the painting the title, *How vast it all is.*' She sits down at the table again. There's a pause.

'I think you may be right. I've tried so hard to capture my sensation of awe in the face of the immensity outside my front door and I knew it hadn't worked. Thank you.' The doctor seems moved.

'That was a really tasty meal,' Dee says to compliment her. 'Thank you. If you've got a right hand rubber glove I could help with the dishes. You've done all the driving and cooking.'

'From the look of your pale face you've done enough for today. You could sit here or in your bedroom.'

'I think I need to lie down, if that's okay with you. I didn't get much sleep on the way up.' She doesn't say that it will be a relief to get away from her guardian for a few hours. The doctor looks as if she's disappointed. Is she lonely living here by herself? She wears a wedding ring. Where's her husband?

There's an en-suite shower room with a toilet and washbasin for Dee's use. The bedroom is painted white and has a stained wooden floor. Dee assumes that the rugs woven in natural colours are also the work of her hostess/guardian/keeper. The double bed, wardrobe, chest of drawers, bookcase and bedside table are pine. There's a comfy armchair. Then she gasps with astonishment. The quilted bedcover! It's the most beautiful Log Cabin arrangement of brilliant colours she's ever seen.

'Did you make this?' she asks incredulously.

'Yes. Margaret came to stay with me for a month when my husband died. She saw to it that I had a "gainful occupation" as she called it, before she left.'

So Doctor Hunter lived alone because her husband was dead.

'It's so precise. Were you by any chance a surgeon doctor?'

'I was an orthopaedic surgeon.'

Dee studies the quilt. 'I can't get over it! You must be wonderfully creative to make a beautiful work of art like this.'

'Nonsense!'

'I'm not sure. It could be a topic for students. *"Are fabulous combinations of colour the work of a beautiful mind? Discuss."* The idea amuses her and she laughs. 'The topic for next week will be, *"Can an ugly heart bring forth beauty? Discuss."* I must fold it over the end of the bed. Will I be warm enough without it?'

'Why can't you leave it where it is?'

That is a difficult question. Dee feels that she has to keep the intensely personal handicraft of this unfriendly woman, beautiful though it is, away from her taut nerves. She's already strung up and talking too freely. Honesty is the best policy.

'Because I feel that you are stitched into every inch of the quilt and you would be too near me.'

'What a notion! Turn it back then. There are more blankets in the bathroom cupboard.'

'Thank you.' But she sees the doctor shiver and the doubt that crosses her face. For all she knows, Dee could be mad. Her friend Margaret might not have made an accurate assessment of the prisoner's character. Dee walks over to the window and looks out at the view.

'I'm not mad,' she says quietly, 'at least not more than the bit nutty they say goes with being artistic. My mother-in-law wrote that I was mad in her suicide note.'

'There was a suicide note?'

'Yes.'

'Wasn't it used as evidence?'

'My husband burnt it.'

'Good God!'

'This is going to happen all my life isn't it? I'll always be the woman who was accused of murdering her mother-in-law. There'll be no escape from the gossip for me, for my children or for my family. To think that in the past I've concerned myself as to whether people liked me! With one false accusation and a hideous photograph in the paper the world has turned against me.'

Dee faces her. 'You needn't be afraid of me Doctor Hunter. Until last week I've only ever killed insects that bite because they find me tasty, and slugs because they eat the vegetables I try to grow. Prisoners attacked me and I fought back. It's the only time I've been violent. It was an instinctive desire to save my life, so that I could stay in one piece until it was time for me to return to my children.

'I kept my spirits up most of the time, during the two weeks in prison, because the whole situation seemed unbelievably absurd. I didn't respond to the verbal abuse. I suffered the sex because it was preferable to the alternative rough treatment. All the time my spirit was somewhere above what was happening, hanging on to my sense of fun and hope. That's gone now and I see you're even afraid of the way I talk.'

She walks over to the door and tries the lock. 'You could lock me in Doctor Hunter. I can't bear the thought of you being afraid of me. I'd be glad of a beaker in my room so that I can get a drink of water.'

'Did Margaret lock you in?'

Dee stares at her in disbelief. 'Margaret! Margaret lock me in?' Tears blind her and she answers vehemently as despair and anger well up in her. 'Margaret is the personification of love. I don't know why...but she totally accepted me. She bathed me and treated me gently. She woke in the night to see if I was all right. She's one of those rare adults who's not afraid to love.' Her voice rises hysterically, – 'and Frances and Barry, they were both kind. They didn't believe I'd murdered anyone. But lock me in Doctor Hunter, not just for your safety but for mine too. This farce has become unbearable.' She chokes with emotion. 'If I hadn't fought for my life, I'd be dead now and none of you would have to be bothered about me. Tonight I wouldn't even try to defend myself.'

'Get ready for bed,' Doctor Hunter says firmly.

'No! Drive me to a public phone box and I'll ring the police. You can leave me there and they can come and collect me. I won't give away any names.'

Dee sees her hesitate. The idea of getting rid of her newcomer is probably very tempting.

'We'll think about it tomorrow. You'd better spend the rest of today in bed.'

Dee doesn't know what the tablets are that the doctor gives her to take. They knock her out. It's eight o'clock in the evening when Doctor Hunter wakes her with a mug of warm milk, some toast and honey and more tablets. She staggers to the toilet and falls back into bed. She opens her eyes once and sees that the doctor is sitting in the armchair by the window, still holding the empty mug and plate. It's nice to have someone there; like the special times when she was ill and her mother lit a fire in the bedroom and came to sleep with her.

## Monday 1st June

On Monday morning, there's no reference to her distressed behaviour of the previous day. She's listless and dozy after taking sedatives.

'Put on this dressing gown and come through for your breakfast,' she's told. It's a big warm tartan dressing gown. 'My husband's,' Doctor Hunter says when she sees Dee's enquiring look.

Dee's eyes light up when she smells the stone-ground oatmeal porridge, with a liberal sprinkling of soft brown sugar. Porridge is her family's staple breakfast but stone-ground oatmeal tastes much more delicious. After breakfast, she dries the dishes and keeps a close eye on where everything belongs. She means to give as much help as she can.

She returns to her room and sits on the bed. Doctor Hunter may not have referred to the subject of her return to prison but Dee's mind is busy with the idea. Perhaps Doctor Hunter doesn't want to disappoint Margaret and is unwilling to initiate the move. In that case she must take responsibility for the departure herself. She would need her guardian to be out of the house for a few hours so that she could get far enough away to find a public phone box, one that's not connected with this area.

There's a shelf of Ordinance maps in the bookcase. She kneels on the floor and spreads out the Map 9 sheet. Isolated homesteads are situated between here and the nearest village of Tongue. She couldn't walk up to any of them and ask to use their phone to call the Police! The journey would mean a walk of about twelve miles to Tongue, unless there's a phone box en route. Eight years since she walked a distance of twelve miles. She only has sandals but she could wear two pairs of socks. In a few days her ribs will be less painful. She replaces the map. She'll have to wait until Doctor Hunter drives to Thurso and it isn't going to happen today. She lies on the bed and falls asleep.

After lunch, Dee walks on the beach. She stands for ages at the water's edge. When she looks back at the cottage she sees that she's being watched. It's miserable of her not to assure Doctor Hunter that she's no intention of drowning herself. She's not proud of her mean spirited attitude toward her hostess. The initial lack of welcome has wakened her resentment. She's angry about the whole situation and chooses to shut the doctor out.

If the waves are quiet, the incessant movement soothes her restlessness. On days when they're a churning, crashing force she glories in their power. Her pain and suffering seem slight in the face of that immensity. She enjoys the wind whipping through her hair and tearing at her trouser legs. The elements are more powerful than human concerns. They lift her out of her helplessness.

She doesn't tell Doctor Hunter that she finds comfort in letting her mind transport her to her familiar and comfortable home life, to her children. Three weeks and four days have passed since she saw her beloved Thea; Thea with a satchel on her back, confident and happy to go to school with her pal, smiling and waving goodbye to her mum. What would Thea feel when she arrived home that Thursday? And Maddy's short legs carrying her upstairs to pack her pink rucksack, happy to be off on a jaunt to Granny and Granddad's, vaguely aware that something wasn't right with her mum.

What can she take back as presents? Bought presents are out of the question – no money, no shops. Shells are the answer. When the tide ebbs, she searches along the beach and begins a collection on the windowsill, left side for Maddy, right for Thea.

She adds beautiful stones and interesting shapes of driftwood. Doctor Hunter provides varnish for her to enhance the colours.

The enforced idleness is strange. She indulges in romantic daydreams but they're all confused. Her well rehearsed stories won't materialise. There's a divorce ahead and this time she's determined to go through with it.

Then there's Tracy Manners and the fact that she let herself enjoy the sex. Does it mean that she's a lesbian, bi-sexual? Is she interested in a relationship with another man? The only person that has attracted her attention in ages is The Penny and she's out of bounds – also she's a peevish woman! She'd no need to be so officious last Thursday, just because she saw her privileged prisoner talking to Mary Burns. She admitted as much to Doctor Tupman. She was probably having a bad day, pre-menstrual tension or lover problems with the Monica that was mentioned. So what? That Thursday was a bad day for quite a few inmates at Stonebridge.

The fact that the beautiful clothes she's wearing every day were chosen by The Penny, contributes to an imagined closeness with the woman. No harm in that. She wonders whether The Penny and the Vice-Principal of Deanswood have hit it off.

No, Dee has no success with her romantic daydreams.


## Wednesday 3ʳᵈ June

After breakfast she's ordered to sit down. 'We'll have that dressing off your forehead.'

'Oh help! You don't want to look at that scar!'

'I've seen more scars than you've had hot dinners. The air needs to get to the wound.' She peels the plaster off gingerly and Dee refrains from her, "Ow! Ouch!" routine under the hands of this professional woman.

'Nice job. Who did it?'

'Doctor Tupman.'

'She's good. I remember her and her husband Mark. He's tarred with the same medical zeal as my husband…was.' She stops abruptly and picks up an instrument.

'Those stitches will have to come out. Are you getting any headaches? A blow that cut your forehead like that could have cracked your skull.'

'I don't know about my skull. I was abducted from the X Ray Department and assume that the x rays went to the prison hospital. My head aches a bit at times.' Dee wonders if she's fishing to know how she got the injury. Some uncomfortable minutes later the tightness and pricking sensations in the wound disappear with the stitches. 'Thank you very much, Doctor Hunter. My head feels freer without the dressing.'

She sets off for the beach but the postie arrives as she opens the door. None of the letters will be for her and she can't write to anyone because of the telltale postmarks. As he mounts his bike the postie says, 'Is Mistress Hunter fine the day?' She nods and says, 'Yes,' frightened in case he recognises her. Doctor Hunter comes out for the mail.

'I thought he might recognise me from the photograph in the paper.'

'The photograph you brought up in your bag?'

'You looked in my bag?'

'I searched your bag,' she says, with no form of apology.

Dee finds the information discomfiting, – that anyone should be suspicious of the contents of her property!

'If you look in the mirror,' Doctor Hunter adds, 'you'll see that your face today has little resemblance to that photograph.' Tears of relief threaten. Dee turns away. 'I notice you don't wear a watch.'

'It's at the prison, with my other possessions.'

'Wear this one,' she says and pulls a handsome watch, with a large clear face, out of her pocket. 'It isn't needed now.'

Dee looks at her ashamed. This kindness, when she's so unfriendly toward her benefactor. It can't be easy for the doctor to part with her husband's watch. Dee's discomfort is obvious. She tries to say thank you but is prevented by a dismissive wave of the doctor's hand, a wave perfected after years of being a hospital consultant? The doctor takes her mail inside and Dee walks slowly and thoughtfully down to the beach.

# WEEK FIVE

Dee's ears prick up during their Wednesday evening meal. Doctor Hunter mentions a visit to Thurso on Thursday, to keep a dentist's appointment and do some shopping.

It's what Dee is waiting for. She knows that if she stays any longer in this beautiful place she'll never summon up the courage to leave. She's continually uncomfortable in Doctor Hunter's company and unhappy with her own truculent attitude. Her arrival has disrupted the doctor's peaceful life and all she has done is use the poor woman as a butt for her anger. Her heart isn't light as she tells herself she must go.

A list of necessaries is firmly fixed in her mind. Outwardly she's cool and collected but her heart's beating wildly. She's never been so loath to carry out a purpose. The minute the Jeep is out of hearing she hurries, panting with anxiety, to pack a small rucksack with a bottle of water, a cheese roll, a Penguin biscuit and a few Marie biscuits. The explanatory note she's composed in advance.

*Thank you very much Doctor Hunter for your kind hospitality. I've borrowed a rucksack which I will return some day. I think it would be better for everybody if I finish serving my three month remand sentence. I'll phone the police from a public phone box. Sincerely Dee*

She anchors the note to the kitchen table with the watch. That brings tears. It was kindly given. She's never owned a good watch but it doesn't seem right to keep it.

Crying before she starts out doesn't bode well. She's never been a weepy person. She would have said she was tough and could cope with any situation. This prison experience has changed all that. Hopefully, she can steady up when she's on her way. She borrows a cloth hat from the hooks in the hall and pulls it well down, ostensibly as protection from the sun, but really so that it hides the gash on her forehead and her wet eyes.

She walks quickly, taking the foot-path round the outskirts of the village. Once she's out on the main road she strides along. The moor of turf and heather stretches away on her left until it reaches the foot of the distant hills. To her right there are views of the sea. When the road curves inland, the terrain rises up sharply. It's quiet and lonely. She feels shut in. There's just the slap of her sandals on the tarmac as her legs move automatically – and the sound of her sobs.

She stands back when the occasional car approaches and acknowledges the drivers' greetings with a feeble wave. She drinks as she walks and eats a biscuit. When she judges it must be lunchtime, she sits at the roadside to eat her cheese roll. A car slows to a standstill beside her. Her heart leaps into her mouth and she scrambles awkwardly to her feet. She notices the driver's open necked, green check shirt and his brown arm resting on the window ledge. His smile is friendly but he's obviously curious. Dee wipes her hand across her cheeks hoping to remove the traces of tears.

'Can I offer you a lift?'

She's thought about this eventuality. She looks back along the road as though expecting to see a car appear. 'My lift should be arriving any minute,' she says. 'Thank you for the offer.'

The car drives off.

Refusing the lift increases her sense of loneliness and renews her misery. Should she have accepted the lift? Has she been unnecessarily cautious? The sun disappears behind a cloud and a chill breeze makes her shiver – she reckons that the tide must have turned. She'll keep warm if she walks quickly.

She must have covered another mile when the first raindrops start to fall. She stares about fearfully, seeing the bleak landscape and wondering why this journey seemed so important a few hours ago. What is she doing, tramping along an empty road, in the Highlands of Scotland, looking for a telephone box and hoping to get herself back into prison? She set off with such purpose. Is it likely that this venture will give her access to her children?

They're hundreds of miles away and there's still no sign of the village of Tongue. Doubt sets in.

She sees a tumbledown shieling set back from the road. Perhaps a little rest will clear her head and help her to renew her efforts. She crouches in the doorway with her head on her knees. Does she hope that Doctor Hunter will come and find her? Not really. She's past caring what happens to her. Whoever finds her in this predicament will have no difficulty in believing that she's an escaped prisoner. She'll be back inside in a jiffy. She remembers a chilling TV film, about an unprepared walker in Arctic conditions. He sat down, defeated, and waited to die. Dee is defeated.

'Come along young woman. Let's have you up.' The voice breaks through her semi-consciousness. Strong arms help her to stand. 'My name's Doctor Gillespie. What're you doing here?'

She can't think of an evasive answer. 'I'm an... es... s...caped prisoner,' she gets out through chattering teeth. 'I wanted... to get to a ph...phone box... and turn myself in.'

'That's not very funny! This is Elspeth Hunter's rucksack. My wife gave it to her. Now let's be hearing the truth.'

'It is the truth.'

'Good God woman! What has Doctor Hunter to do with an escaped prisoner?'

'Her friend Margaret sent me to stay with her.'

'Well, I ken Margaret fine. We'd better get you back and I'll hope for the full story.'

He wraps her in a woollen rug and tucks her in the passenger seat of his car. The miles that have taken all morning to walk, speed by in a few minutes. He knocks briefly on the door of Hunter's Lodge, opens it and calls out, 'Elspeth, it's Don.' Dee follows and stands limply in the hall. Elspeth doesn't answer. Through the open door of her bedroom they see her lying back against her pillows.

'Elspeth, what ails you?' Then he sees the open bottle of pills. 'You've taken your tablet?' He screws the top on the bottle and returns it to the drawer in her bedside table.

She nods, – her face wan. 'I'll be all right in a few minutes.'

'I've brought back a runaway. Get those wet clothes off,' Doctor Gillespie directs at Dee. 'Hot water bottles, Elspeth?'

'They're on the back of the pantry door.'

'I'll make us all a cup of tea in a minute.'

He follows Dee into the bedroom and assists with peeling off her wet clothes. He hands her a towel to dry her front and proceeds to rub briskly at her hair and back. She's in bed, tingling and shivering, smothered by blankets, heated with two hot water bottles and drinking from a mug of tea, within ten minutes.


Doctor Gillespie carries a tray into Elspeth's room and draws the door to. Dee can hear their conversation across the echoing, narrow stone-flagged hallway.

'Now Elspeth, let's be having this story. Archie told me you'd a visitor at Hunter's Lodge and that she has injuries. I see her arm's in plaster. So, is it true that she's an escaped prisoner?'

'Her name's Deanna Livesey. She's the woman accused of murdering her mother-in-law. Margaret and her family helped her to escape from hospital and asked me to look after her. They thought she wouldn't be traced up here because it's so out of the way. She's to return for her Hearing at the end of July.'

'That's an awful imposition Elspeth.'

'I didn't feel I could say no. Remember how good Margaret was to me when Doug died. I felt I owed her this favour. I wasn't keen on the idea and I suppose it showed in my attitude. I succeeded in alienating Dee from the word go. She won't call me Elspeth and I asked her to.'

'Has she behaved well?'

'Oh yes. I can't fault her politeness and she's quick to help about the place. But she won't talk to me. She wanders off and spends hours by herself. I know she's grieving for her children, two young daughters I believe. She's rather unusual. I'd written her off as useless company at our first meal and then she made some surprisingly accurate comments about one of my paintings. She also made some extraordinary remarks about my needlework.'

'Such as?'

'You must be a beautifully creative person to make such a wonderful work of art.'

Dee hears the doctor laugh. 'That would give you a shock, private person that you are. What did you say?'

'I said "nonsense."'

'Aye...so you would. Was that the end of it?'

'No, she threw the idea open for debate. "*Are fabulous combinations of colours and shape the work of a beautiful mind? Discuss.*" Did you ever!'

Dee hears the doctor laugh even louder.

'I thought she might be mad.'

'I hardly think so Elspeth. We could have a philosophical discussion on those points.'

'She wanted me to contact the police and send her back on the first night. I'd have been glad to get rid of her but I kept thinking that I would let Margaret down.'

'How did she get that scar? Is Margaret convinced that she's innocent?'

'You know that Margaret's daughter Jane is the governor of a women's prison. When Dee was admitted to prison, Jane interviewed her and thought she was innocent. She shared the information with her family. A fortnight later there must have been a fight at the prison. Dee's been hit with something hard. Soft-hearted Margaret went to visit her in hospital, decided Dee was in a dangerous nervous state and got her son and his friends to kidnap her from hospital.'

'My God Elspeth, I know Margaret's a strong minded woman but what a foolhardy venture! And this Dee, fancy her having to go through that experience if she's done nothing wrong.'

'I know, and I've done nothing to help her. I've been quietly satisfied with my ordered world since Doug died; lonely sometimes, you know what it's like. But I've kept occupied and content. The first time I'm asked to help in an unfamiliar situation, I fail miserably.'

'Mistress Hunter, you've given this young woman a safe retreat. You stop berating yourself.'

'I got a shock Don, when I got back from Thurso this afternoon and found her gone. I didn't know she was so resourceful, or thoughtful. She was prepared to walk for miles to avoid suspicion falling on me. I gave her Doug's watch and she left it behind. I thought, "Well, she's taken the decision into her own hands and removed her unwelcome presence," then I realized that I'd been enjoying making meals for us both. I bought strawberries and cream in Thurso, thinking she would like them for tea. Margaret warned me that her nerves and emotions are fragile. She trusted me to take care of her... Don, what would Doug have thought of me, of someone wanting to run away from me? I suddenly wasn't sure what to do and that's when my heart kicked in.'

'Are you feeling better now?'

'Yes, I'm fine and very grateful to you. You brought her back before I could get round to it.'

'I saw her this morning on the road about five miles from from Tongue, and asked her if she wanted a lift. I was very puzzled because she'd obviously been crying. I couldn't hang about because I was meeting Doctor Metcalfe at the hotel. He's standing in for me while I go down for a couple of weeks to stay with Alastair and family.'

'Will you remove Dee's plaster when you get back, please?'

'I will indeed Doctor Hunter, if you'll come and help me.'

There's a little silence and Dee wonders how friendly these two doctors are. He mentioned a wife in connection with the rucksack.

'You don't need any help Don Gillespie, but I'll oblige.'

'Of course you will. Give me a wee non-professional hug and I'll leave you to have a rest. I'll look in later in the week.'

He walks into Dee's bedroom and checks that she's warm before he leaves.

Doctor Hunter is standing by Dee's bed when she wakes later that afternoon. She indicates that Dee is to hold out her wrist. Once more she becomes the owner of a handsome watch.

'Shall you get up for some tea?'

'Yes please.'

'And, by the way, that's the last we'll hear of returning to prison.' She waits to see if the words have sunk in. 'It's not an option. Your main aim is to get well. In a few weeks you'll be back at home with your children and domestic responsibilities. I can't see that a further spell in prison would fulfil that aim. Just set your mind positively to getting through the next few weeks.'

'I will Doctor Hunter.'

'Good...and the name's Elspeth!'

'Okay Elspeth,' she says with a shy smile. Before she goes through to the living room, she takes the patchwork quilt out of the wardrobe, unfolds it, and spreads the magnificent colours across her bed.

# WEEK SIX

Friday 12th June

Dee is not comfortable with Elspeth at first, knowing that she's caused her to have a heart tremor. Elspeth won't hear any mention of it, waives her apologies with, "Past, yesterday, forget it." Dee is only too glad to forget it. Listening to Elspeth, as she confided in Doctor Gillespie last night, gave her the insight into Elspeth's feelings that she needed – into her vulnerability. It's not in Dee's nature to be reserved. She's missed talking, so she opens the conversation.

'When I took your rucksack, I wondered how I could get it back to you,' she says with a guilty grin, 'and your water bottle.'

'The bottle didn't matter but the rucksack is precious. It was my birthday present from Alice Gillespie in 1967. She died before my next birthday.' Dee waits to see if she'll say more. Has Elspeth missed talking too?

'Doug and I always wanted to settle up here. We had these two cottages knocked into one and Don and Alice Gillespie liked to come for a "comfy evening" as they called it. It's very cosy in the winter with the stove lit and we'd play cards or just natter. Alice did beautiful embroidery and knitting so we were each interested in our efforts in the craft direction. Don and Doug's talk was mainly medical. I was consulted if Don had a problem with one of his patients. My foolish Doug wanted to do one more consultancy in Africa four years ago. He caught an infection and there was no cure on hand. He died over there and was brought home. He's buried here in the churchyard.'

Archie arrives with the post and saves Elspeth from saying more.

Dee is struck by this reality of Elspeth suddenly becoming a widow. A good marriage, – years with a partner, followed by separation and the finality of death. Whatever must it be like to have your heart's-love die? She'll be spared that sorrow now. Betrayed love has already torn at her heart. Once she knew for certain that Jon was having an affair with Sarah, she spent every minute alone, listening to soulful music, scarcely able to breathe because of the intense pain – wondering what to do. She hadn't believed in heartache till then. She's not willing to go through that again in a hurry. Days can jog on with familiarity and then suddenly, change and shock. How did Elspeth cope with the suddenness? Margaret said that her friend in Scotland was lively and they'd had lots of fun. Elspeth seems very serious and dour. Was it Doug's death that took the fun out of her?

The accusation of murder has violently affected her own life; it's caused a shake-up of her behaviour and attitudes. Her "familiarity" has gone up in smoke. She hopes it will be part of eventual enlightenment, having always believed that "good" can come from any situation – a belief that is being thoroughly put to the test.

Elspeth drives off to see a friend who lives further along the coast. Dee won't be hearing how Alice Gillespie died today.

'You suggested that I introduce a figure into my seascape,' Elspeth says after lunch. 'I'd like you to pose for a photograph at the water's edge.'

'It's a bit chilly. Margaret didn't pack any woollies.'

'That's okay. She knows I'm well stocked.'

Dee, wearing a huge roll neck sweater in soft wool and one of Elspeth's pleated skirts, walks with Elspeth down to the beach. Dee poses, as instructed, by the water's edge. The wide jumper sleeves hide her stiff arm. Photos are taken of her front, back and sides with the skirt flaring up in the wind. Her hair flies about. They laugh and she puts up her hand to hold it down. Elspeth takes a close up shot of her head and shoulders.

After the photo shoot, Elspeth disappears into her bathroom-cum-dark room. 'Too far into Thurso every time I want a photo developing,' she says, – 'that's why I created my own darkroom and produce my own photographs.'

Dee sits on the garden wall and waits. She's surprised at the speed with which Elspeth returns and hands her the results of the photo shoot.

'Wow!' she says, 'I look…'

'Yes, you do. You look lovely,' Elspeth finishes for her. 'I'll send one of these to Hattersley.'

'Jane might see it.'

'No problem, Jane knows you're here,' she says in a matter of fact voice.

'Jane knows! When…?'

'The day you arrived.'

'Why didn't you tell me?'

'You weren't exactly approachable, and in your wild state I thought the news might add to your anxiety.'

'How did she find out?'

'She saw Barry leave with someone in the passenger seat of his car and asked questions. Margaret wanted her to know you were safe.'

'I wonder what she said.'

'Margaret said Jane went mad. She was furious with her, raged and called her a well-intentioned, misguided, interfering woman. Jane fears for the family of course. Margaret has put her in a dreadful position. If the truth about the kidnap comes out she'll lose her job and Barry and Jim will be indicted. She stormed off to her flat and hasn't been home to Hattersley since.'

'Oh dear, Margaret will be upset.'

'Margaret can't expect Jane to behave in any other way. It was evidently a risk she was prepared to take. She probably trusts her relationship with Jane to come right when we've got you out of the way.'

'Thank you very much! Not too long to wait for any of you. Do you think the police are watching the family? Is the phone tapped?'

'There's really no reason why the police would suspect the Pennyfields family. Margaret doesn't phone me from Hattersley, just to be safe. Fran had a brainwave the night you left. She and Margaret set off early on the Sunday and made phone calls to your family, and to me, from public phone boxes in Derbyshire and Cheshire then drove to Blackpool for the night. They do things in style. Margaret's husband Hugh liked big cars. You would likely see Frances chauffeur Margaret in the Daimler? That's the last car Hugh bought.'

'Yes, I saw the Daimler. Jane and Barry are following in their father's footsteps in that respect. Jane's Jag is a beauty.'

'I've heard.'

'Has anyone been suspected of kidnapping me?'

'No. Enquiries were made and an elderly lady, who lives opposite Lineham Park, said she saw you get out of one car and into another. She thought it was odd that you were in a kimono, "a very pretty kimono" she said, but she was so impressed by Barry's courteous manner toward you that she thought everything must be all right. She dismissed the incident and got on with her housework.'

They're both amused.

'She didn't name the cars?'

'She only recognises her son's Beetle; said one of the cars was a greeny colour but couldn't be of more help.'

'I'm glad Jane knows that I didn't plan the escape. She made my imprisonment as easy as she could by giving me a gardening job, where I could work on my own. She was really interested in the garden.'

'Jane interested in gardening! I don't think so! Jane doesn't know one plant from another.'

'Yes, I know it was Margaret and Barry who provided the plants and the advice, but she did go to the market and buy trays of annuals. It was her day off too.'

'Hmm... That does *not* sound like Jane! You're sure it isn't you that she's interested in?'

'ME!'

'She has been known to be romantically involved with a lady friend.'

'Yes, I gathered that, but not me.'

'Why not?'

'Elspeth, I'm still married. Besides which, she and I wouldn't get on. We function in different worlds.'

'You think?'

Elspeth is leafing through a photograph album and comes across a photo of Jane on the beach, wearing the same woollen jumper.

'Isn't she lovely?' Dee can't help saying.

'That's what I've just said about you.'

'I'm not in the same class.'

'You're in your own class. You haven't got a crush on her by any chance? You've gone quite pink. Oh I've noticed madam! Jane's name has been conspicuous by its absence since the day you arrived. I know you were interviewed by her, and that you met her on a number of occasions, but you haven't once mentioned her since you left Hattersley.'

Dee doesn't answer. She can't. Elspeth's queries stir excited feelings and she doesn't know what to make of them. Elspeth sees that she's perplexed and suggests a walk before tea.

# WEEK EIGHT

Saturday 4<sup>th</sup> July

Dee has been looking forward to today. The plaster is coming off her arm. They've to be at Donald's surgery at nine o'clock. He got back yesterday from his holiday with his son and family, who live in Edinburgh.

'We'll go to the surgery in the Jeep,' Elspeth says at breakfast. 'There'll be a lot of visitors around. It's the height of the holiday season and there are the Games this afternoon. We don't want to take the chance of you being recognised.'

On the way, she points out the Games' field which is a hive of activity. Dee catches sight of the cordoned off area with the wooden stage for the dancers and pipers. The caber is lying there, waiting to be tossed. Tents and Portaloos are ready to provide their various functions.

'I'd like to have gone to the Games. I used to enjoy them when we camped at Morar in our school holidays. I won five-bob in the races that follow the main events.'

'Are those the holidays that developed your appreciation of stone-ground oatmeal porridge?'

'Yes. Mum and the three of us children ate porridge for breakfast every day but the oatmeal that the village shopkeeper scooped out of a sack, in the little shop in Morar, was the best we'd ever tasted. Our tent was pitched just below the railway station. I used to prepare the porridge on the primus stove, leave it on a low light for Mum to look after, and then run round the headland for the milk. If the tide was in, I had to run over the headland. Miss McClellan had one cow and sometimes I had to wait for her to milk it.'

'Things have changed since then. You'll have to come back again another year if you want to see these Games.'

'You'll be glad to see the back of me at the end of the month. I'll just be a memory of your interrupted summer.'

She laughs, but Elspeth is thoughtful.

Don looks brown and well. The family has spent most of the fortnight at North Berwick, a change of coast and sea-side. He soon removes the plaster from Dee's arm.

'I'm disappointed,' she says when she tries to flex the arm. 'I didn't think it would be so stiff and painful.'

'What do you expect after it's been rigid, encased in plaster for six weeks, impatient woman,' Elspeth chivvies.

'You'll have to get Elspeth to massage it for you.' Don smiles mischievously but Elspeth's reproving look silences him. He laughs. He's good fun. Elspeth could do with lightening up. Don is her idea of a stereotype country doctor, friendly and interested. He's tall, like her memories of her maternal grandpa in his Harris Tweed jackets and with the same twinkle in his eye.

'I've one or two places to call Donald. Can I leave Dee with you for a few minutes?'

'Why don't we meet next door at eleven for coffee? Laura McGregor has filled my tins with biscuits and cakes. I'll be the size of a house if I eat them all myself.' Donald's surgery comprises two rooms at the side of his house. Elspeth agrees with the arrangement. 'Now young woman, shall we go for a little walk?'

'I might be seen.'

'Not the path we'll take.'

They leave the surgery together, Dee is nervous. She can't forget that she's an escaped prisoner.

'Don't worry lass. Any new face hereabouts causes a stir. Everybody knows everybody else. If the doctor was seen walking down the street with a young woman on a normal day it would give rise to gossip. We won't be as obvious this morning with all the visitors about. This afternoon I'll wander over to the playing field, in case a doctor is needed. My services come in handy when over-enthusiastic competitors strain muscles or take a tumble.'

Donald takes Dee down an alley that cuts between the houses on the main-street and leads to a quiet little churchyard. They skirt the graves dating back to the eighteenth century and walk over to the more recent burials. They stand silently by Alice Mary Gillespie's grave and then Dee follows Donald and reads on a tombstone, *Douglas Arthur Hunter 1966*, the reason for Elspeth's solitary existence.

They squeeze through a stile in the stone wall and stroll along the cliff path. The landscape is bare, just a few windswept and gnarled hawthorn trees. Dee misses the softness of large, leafy deciduous trees.

Donald stops. 'This is where my wife died,' he says sadly. 'She tripped when she was near the edge of the cliff and the strong wind carried her forward.'

Elspeth never got round to telling Dee how Donald's wife had died and she hadn't liked to ask. Now she understands why. She looks at the sheer drop, with here and there jagged edges protruding from the cliff edge. She imagines Alice Gillespie precipitated to her sudden death. Donald would be standing on this spot crazed with shock.

'How did she come to be so near the edge Don?'

'I blame myself, Dee. Alasdair, his wife and the bairns were over for a few days. We wanted to go for a short walk after lunch hoping to tire little Jan so that she would have an afternoon nap. It was really too windy to be on the cliff path and I should have realised it. Jan was excited with her walking and the wind carried her toward the cliff edge faster than was good for her little legs. Alice and Fiona raced to catch her. Fiona got there first and swept her up into her arms but Alice stumbled on the uneven ground and fell forward. I still see her with her arms flailing and her skirt billowing...accidents Dee...I've been called out to so many. I would never have believed that this could happen to my family.'

'Can we move away from here Don? It's too dreadful.' A few weeks ago, she was listening to Mary Burns telling her about the accident that changed her life – a few months ago, it was her own daughter that was knocked down.

They sit together on a nearby wooden bench, sited to view the sunset.

'I come here nearly every day...I seem to be drawn here.'

'Oh Donald...' she begins but doesn't know how to continue. 'Is it a good idea to renew your grief every day?'

'I feel that Alice is here.'

'Do you think that she wants to be where she died?' Dee blurts out. He doesn't answer. 'Your grief might be keeping her spirit from going on to wherever spirits go after death.'

They sit in silence. She hopes she hasn't offended him. After what seems like a long time he checks with his watch.

'We'd better get back to meet up with Elspeth.'

They return, walking over the springy turf without speaking. Elspeth is waiting for them. Dee is relieved to hear Don say, 'Your charge has been helping me to set my mind straight but we won't talk about it now. Let's have coffee.'


'I see Laura McGregor is keeping house for you very well.' Elspeth says, nosing round Don's lounge while the coffee is percolating. 'Alice's embroidered cushions look as fresh as the day she finished them but your pipes have stolen on to the hearth, instead of being in the conservatory, and your piles of medical journals and *Wild Times* magazines threaten to take over your living space.'

He grins like a naughty boy. He's fine and handy with the tray but welcomes Elspeth's offer to serve their drinks.

'I've poured us a dash of rum; it goes well with morning coffee. I'm still in holiday mood. Did you hear about Archie's girl Moira? She's competing in the dancing this afternoon. She left her tartan sash lying and the dog chewed it. His wife Martha has had to drive to Thurso for a new one. Elspeth, you've got a tartan rig I remember. How about going as my partner to the Ceilidh tonight?'

'I don't know. It would mean leaving Dee.'

'Gosh! I don't mind. It'll be great for you to go Elspeth. I'm jealous of course. I'd love to dance at the Ceilidh.'

'Can you do the Scottish Dancing Dee?'

'Yes. I danced as lady number two in the University Scottish Country Dancing team. I still have my ghillies. What I would like to do Elspeth, is have a session with your records this evening. May I please?'

'You may, as long as you put them back in the right places. It took me ages to organise them.'

'Don't worry, I will. I've been well trained. Jon's catalogue of his antiquarian books and records is second to none.'

'Everybody's happy then,' Don says. 'I'll pick you up at seven forty-five Elspeth.'


## Saturday evening

Elspeth appears when Dee is on her knees by the bookcase, choosing her music programme for the evening. She's written titles on pieces of paper and carefully slotted them into the spaces she's left.

'You look very fetching in your white blouse Elspeth. I like your diamante earrings and that tartan skirt will twirl nicely when you swing.'

'Good gracious, you'll never get through all those records in an evening!'

'I shall select the bands that I want to listen to. Don't fuss just because you're nervous.'

'I'm not nervous. Well, perhaps I am a little. I've always liked Don but since Alice died I've deliberately kept out of his way because I'm afraid of gossip. You know the sort of thing, "Widow Hunter chases newly-widowed village doctor." Most of the women in the village are in love with him. It's your fault madam that we've caught up with each other, you and your running away and your broken arm.'

'Don't complain, you might live to thank me one day. Go and enjoy yourself, if you can. He might be a bad dancer and tread on your toes.'

'Oh no, he's a good dancer,' she says with conviction and from that Dee surmises that she's danced with him in former days – when the four of them attended ceilidhs.

They hear his Land Rover pull up outside.


Dee lies on the couch and listens to a side of Wagner's *Tristan and Isolde*. This is the type of sad romantic music that she likes best. It suits her experience of love, love that is felt but can't work out because of circumstances, or love that dies. She's at the stage where she questions whether love between two people ever lasts. Only three or four of her friends have happy marriages.

She often wonders if seeing the film *Intermezzo,* when she was eleven, undermined her belief in happy-ever-afters. Her aunty Janet took her to the cinema for a treat – or because she wanted company. When unfaithful Leslie Howard returned to his wife, after his affair with Ingrid Bergman, and the front door slowly shut on the family home, Dee wanted to scream out, "How can you have him back when he left you for another woman?" Did that film set a pattern of failed marriage for her?

Has she been lacking in trust, undermining her marriage all the time, because she was afraid that Jon would fancy another woman? No, what was there to trust? She hoped against hope that, when he visited London, he was not sleeping with Hazel, his erstwhile girlfriend – and he was. Mind you, nice presents did arrive after those visits, peace offerings from Liberty's, the red enamel brooch, the black woollen stole, the pewter pendant set with pink stones.

The marriage was probably a failure from the start. It could continue if she was prepared to fulfil her role as dutiful wife and mother, and leave Jon to his own devices. No, she's had enough, and now that his mother is dead she doesn't have to preserve the family home and put up with his infidelity. The front door of her *Intermezzo* home can close and he will be on the other side of it.

She plays a side of *La Traviata*. Poor Violetta! The doomed heroine suits her mood too, though she's no intention of expiring because her marriage is on the rocks. She wonders if there are any operas written about happy love. Operettas yes, *The Merry Widow*. There must be a state where one person says to another, "I love you" and hears the reply, "I love you" and they mean it, believe it and trust themselves to it. Unfortunately, that experience hasn't been charted into her life-path but she'll hang on to her pleasure in fairytales, fantasy and escapism.

She plays Richard Strauss' *Four Last Songs*, continuing to indulge in beautiful melancholy. She used to be able to lie and daydream happy endings, spend hours creating love scenes and working on the dialogue until she had it perfect. She'd review the stories and add to them as a soporific each night. Now she can't conjure up a comforting daydream.

Tracy Manners has got in the way of her sex scenes. She's upset the male-female passion that filled her fantasies. She can't even think of a man she fancies. The only person that she admires is Jane Pennyfields. It's safe to fantasize about someone who's out of reach. If she attempts a daydream about her would it mean that she's a lesbian?

It's eleven-thirty by the time her woe is musically sated. She replaces the records, makes a bedtime drink and takes it through to her bedroom. She doesn't want Elspeth to come home and find her up. The moon is big and bright ,and the sky, this far north is light. There's no one to see her if she doesn't draw the curtains. She undresses and puts on her nighty by moonlight. She's not asleep when she hears Don's vehicle arrive.

The two Ceilidh goers don't come in. Dee sits up in bed and sees them perch on the garden wall, very near to each other. She should lie down and stop peeking but she's curious. They chat for a bit and then they kiss. Wow! But Don gets up and sets off down the path to the beach. Dee kneels on the bed and watches them through the window. Elspeth follows slowly and stands looking at Don. He chucks pebbles into the water, they look like vicious throws. What's eating him? Why is he fed up? Elspeth says something to him and then they're arguing, pacing about their arms going like mad. Don puts his hands on Elspeth's shoulders as though to calm her down and the next minute they're embracing each other. Oh wow, how super!

It's time for her to lie down and mind her own business. She dives under the covers and then comes up for air. She's so excited! How can she sleep after seeing that love embrace? She's so glad for Elspeth but she wants some of that thrill for herself. She wants – a sob catches in her throat and tears prick her eyelids. She wants some of that love in her life. To hell with it! She's going to imagine being in love with Jane Pennyfields, imagine playing pop music and dancing in her arms. Being held against Jane Pennyfields' body and moving to music would be ecstasy.

She must be a lesbian if she thinks and feels like that, – she's proving it to herself. She buries her head under the covers and whispers, 'I'm a lesbian.' But she's been married...and had children, been attracted to some men. What does that make her? She remembered saying to Frances, "I'm a woman. Do I have to have a label?" Tonight she can add, 'I'm a sexual woman who can be attracted to a man or a woman.' Now she thinks about it, hasn't she always looked at women? She's just never thought about them in a sexual context. Now she's so excited that she sits up. No use attempting to sleep.

Sometime later, she hears Don's vehicle drive away and Elspeth tiptoe in. She keeps as still as a mouse. She doesn't want in any way to draw attention to herself on Elspeth's special evening. She waits until Elspeth's in bed and when she thinks she'll be asleep she creeps out in her sandals. The door isn't locked day or night so it's easy to turn the handle and let herself out. She has a great need to move.

She goes down on to the beach and dances in her bare feet. She runs and leaps and stretches her arms out to the moon. She can't open herself widely enough to the feeling of liberation. She feels freed from her doubts and fears. She might be legally in captivity but otherwise she's a free person.

She paddles in the cold water and thinks seriously. She had to get to this point where she can deliberate and make her own decision, not go along (as she has always done) with the opinions of other people. There's no need to say anything to anybody because she's not in a relationship. If she did fall in love with a woman, that's when difficulties would present themselves, – the practical side of introducing her daughters to a woman partner and where would they live? But, she might never meet another partner, male or female. In that case, she'll make as good a life as possible for herself, Thea and Maddy. Her new friends would understand how she's feeling tonight. Barry said she would get it sorted.

She wished that she could talk with her kind math's teacher now. She wondered at the time, about the tall, friendly woman who answered the door when her teacher was ill and she took a posy round to her house. They were probably lesbians, but to outward appearances lived quietly as lady companions. No one in those days mentioned lesbians. From Elspeth's remarks, Dee can tell that she isn't fazed by homosexuality.

Perhaps she'll sleep now. She picks her way carefully up the stony path and closes the garden gate quietly. But there's a light from inside the house and the silhouette of a figure in the doorway. They don't speak. Neither of them feels like talking but they obviously need company. Elspeth heats milk and Dee makes toast and honey. They sit on either side of the kitchen table, stunned by their momentous night. Dee reaches for Elspeth's free hand and she doesn't take it away.


## Sunday 5th July

They're both up early, despite their two in the morning bedtime. Dee smiles when she sees the bottle of massage oil warming on the windowsill in the sunlight. Elspeth is following Doctor Gillespie's suggestion. After breakfast she works on Dee's arm. Her patient says a good few, 'Oh's and 'ouches,' as her muscles are probed by Elspeth's strong fingers.

'And what was all the dancing about for last night, may I ask?'

'You may ask. It was the joy of having two arms that function.'

'Is that so? I take it you danced like that before you had a broken arm?'

'No.'

'So what's the real reason?'

'I haven't asked you what you were doing on the beach last night.' She receives a sharp slap for that remark and her treatment finishes abruptly, but Elspeth's smiling. 'Be careful,' Dee says, 'if you smile as well as having a love affair with Don Gillespie, you'll be in danger of losing your dour-doc image.'

'Dour doctor, is that how you think of me?'

'Well, you aren't a bundle of laughs and Margaret said you used to be good fun – not that anyone would be full of joy to have an escaped prisoner land on their doorstep.' She wondered if she'd gone too far. 'Last night, can't we just say that it was a revelatory experience for both of us, each in our own way of course?' She laughs and escapes into her bedroom out of the way of another slap. She pops her head round the door. 'When are you seeing Don again?'

'He's coming at eleven.'

'I'd like to walk to the other side of the bay and do some drawing.'

'You can borrow my bag with water colour materials and sketch book. Let's pack you some lunch and we'll have our meal at six o'clock. Thank you Dee, we'll have to keep our friendship to ourselves for the time being. Don's house in the village is too public.'

'I'm only sorry that I'm in the way Elspeth. It won't be long before you'll have the unhindered run of your own house. I'll enjoy my day out.'

She carries a rug to sit on, and puts a cardigan, her food and Elspeth's art equipment in a rucksack. The distance across the sandy bay is about three-quarters of a mile. She reaches the far side of the bay and finds a comfortable hollow for a seat, glad she brought the rug because the grass is wiry and it prickles her legs. She sees Don's Land Rover arrive but she's soon absorbed in drawing and it takes her mind off what might be happening at Hunters' Lodge.

The late night and fresh air send her off to sleep after she's eaten. When she wakes, she's content to lie and do nothing. She feels well. Who would have thought that a prison sentence could provide a blissful afternoon like this? She tries not to let the nagging fact, that there are only twenty-two days left before she must leave, spoil her pleasure in the moment.

# WEEK TEN

## Saturday 18th July

They've enjoyed two lovely weeks. Elspeth is happy. She and Don grab a few minutes together whenever they can. He's taken her on some of his inland visits and they've stayed out all day. Last weekend they motored down to somewhere near Lairg for a night in a hotel.

Dee is okay on her own. She works outside now that both of her arms function. Elspeth has logs delivered for the wood burning stove. Dee disappears whenever a delivery man calls; it's better not to be seen, even at this late stage. She stacks the logs, covers them with a tarpaulin and brings in a pile to dry in the log basket. Then there's Elspeth's garden – Elspeth's pursuits have understandably taken her energy away from her garden. Dee is in charge and it's looking good. She has the weeds in the veg patch removed as soon as they appear. The soil is scrubby and stony in the locality but it grows pretty poppies, cornflowers and yellow daisies. When she's finished she sits on the wall and looks at the sea.

Dee likes having a free hand in Elspeth's kitchen. Her guardian is not a great cook and enjoys the meals that Dee prepares. Dee writes the shopping lists. Hopefully she'll be back in her own kitchen soon. She feels that the work is gradually helping her to regain control of her life. A divorce will mean a move to a smaller house and a different kitchen. She will cope with that but what about Thea and Maddy? It will be an upheaval for them, yet it can't have been good for them to live with a mother who was constantly unhappy. Poor kids, it's not their fault that the marriage is breaking.

She's very unsure about the return to her home. How will it work out? It won't be too strange for Thea to see her and Jon sleep apart, after this long absence. Jon can sleep in his mother's bedroom, unless Sarah has a house and he moves in with her.

Maddy isn't aware of what her daddy does because he's been out of the house so frequently in the evenings, or shut away in his study. She doesn't think Maddy will miss him too much. She and Jon can arrange frequent access for the girls.

She would like to go to her mum and dad's at Burylane straight from prison. The school holidays start in the week of her hearing. She hopes someone will take Thea to Burylane. It will be better to have their reunion there. She feels a stab of excitement at the prospect – but there's no certainty.

The weather has broken. The warm spell has continued for weeks and now she and Elspeth are both wearing jumpers because there's driving rain outside and the wind is finding its way through the gap under the door. They can hear the roar of huge Atlantic rollers crashing onto the beach. Dee plans to go treasure hunting in the morning.

The two of them are sitting cosily on the settee in front of the stove, where the dry logs burn with leaping flames. Don has gone to a weekend medical conference in Inverness. They're surrounded by pieces of drawing paper. Dee said she was interested in the alterations that had made Hunters' Lodge a large and accommodating residence. What was it like when the Hunters bought it? Elspeth looked out the architect's plans, photos of before and after, and explains how the changes were made. She asks Dee about her house.

'I haven't seen any plans for our house. The kitchen must have been added at the back of the house because the floors have different levels. Jon and I have to go down two steps to our bedroom.'

'Go on, draw me a floor plan,' Elspeth challenges.

That's reasonably easy but Elspeth wants to know which room the girls sleep in and where Grandma Livesey slept. She insists on Dee positioning the beds and furniture so that she can imagine them all at home. That's not so easy. Dee tends to draw the furniture too small and it seems as though there's loads of floor space. She decides to draw one room at a time to get it right. They do a lot of laughing when they compare Dee's rough sketches with the immaculate professional plans. Elspeth's an awful tease.

'I shan't employ you, should I need any more work doing on the cottage!' she says. 'You make up the fire. I'll fill up our wine glasses.'

Elspeth tidies away the papers.

'I never thought I'd be saying this to you, Deanna Livesey, but I've enjoyed you being here, once we got over the rocky start. I shall miss you. You know...Doug and I rather skated over the question of whether to have children. We were utterly absorbed in our work and each other. Our home was spacious and holidays abroad were a must. It's now that Doug's no longer here that I regret having no one that belongs to me. But look at Margaret! I'm sure she would have loved grandchildren but Julia is dead and it doesn't seem likely that Barry or Jane is going to procreate. Wouldn't grandchildren have loved this beach?'

'And their nice Granny Elspeth, yes they would. Life's not straightforward for anyone is it? I'm as happy as an escaped prisoner could be, with you, and in these wonderful surroundings. I'll be sorry to leave. It will be another dramatic move for me and it's not likely to be the last this year,' she says solemnly.

'I mentioned to Margaret when I phoned, that you would like to go home with your mother if the hearing goes well.'

'Thank you. I'm not sure what will happen after that. How is everybody at Hattersley?'

'In a good state. Jane finally went home for the weekend a fortnight ago. She asked Margaret whether "Operation Livesey Return" was underway and snaffled your photograph off the kitchen notice board.'

'I'm surprised Margaret put it there. No wonder she confiscated it.' She wonders whether the photograph went into a drawer in The Penny's desk or into the waste-paper bin.

'Hm.'

'Are they still expecting me to stay at Hattersley when I get back? Oh, it makes my tum turn over to think about it!'

'Yes, they've big plans for your return. Shopping was mentioned.'

'I can't go out and about!'

'Margaret believes that if you behave as though everything is normal no one will be suspicious and she says you need some new clothes. There was mention of a night in a hotel so that you would be on hand for the courthouse on the Friday morning.'

'Oh gracious, oh Elspeth, I wish I could just stay here! I don't want to face it all.'

'Staying here wouldn't get you back to your girls. Besides, I'm on B & B duty on the fifth of August. My friends, Geoffrey Howell and his wife, come up each year for a fortnight's holiday. Frances and Margaret are due to come in October. Do you think you and the girls would like to visit me next summer?'

'Oh yes! We would love to visit you; that's really something to look forward to, if I'm not in prison.'

Mention of prison always sobers them.

'Will Don mind you having visitors?'

'Don knows them all. Margaret's husband Hugh insisted that she fly up to Inverness to stay with me for a month when Doug died. She met Don then. That was probably one of the reasons I was miserable when I collected you from Thurso station. I'd been sitting in the Jeep, remembering the bleak February day when I waited for Margaret to arrive by train from Inverness. Don's only met the Howells once but he'll get on fine with him and his wife. Geoffrey's a real character, a judge. You'd get a fair chance if Geoffrey was in charge of your Hearing.' The reminder again; Elspeth changes the subject. 'Will you write to me?'

'Yes, I like writing letters. This has been a difficult time for me, not being able to communicate with anyone.'

'And will you phone to let me know the result of the Hearing?'

'I'll phone you immediately if I'm at liberty. If not, Margaret will probably let you know.'

They listen to the music, each alone with her thoughts, until bedtime.

# WEEK TWELVE

## Saturday 25th July

Dee is going to get to Tongue before she leaves. Don and Elspeth want to make her last weekend memorable; they're driving to Tongue to have a meal at the hotel.

Dee follows the road with interest and looks out for the shieling where she rested.

'Bring back memories young lady? Don asks. 'That's where your reprobate lodger was huddled that fateful day Elspeth.'

'If you were a kind polite gentlemen, you wouldn't remind me of my folly and ensuing embarrassment,' Dee retorts. 'I was watching out for the shieling and hoping we'd get past it without comment from you.'

He laughs. The world is very right for him these days.

They park by the little shop in the village which is a mistake. The air is clouded with midges and they have to hurry into the interior of the hotel to escape them. They agree that Dee is best sitting in a chair facing the window so that customers see her back. From their lively conversation no one would guess that there is an escaped prisoner at their table. Lunch is leisurely and delicious. Don sticks to one beer as he's a responsible driver but Elspeth and Dee drink sherry and red wine.

After lunch Don drives them to a beach and they sit on a rug on the grass. Dee soon wanders off to search for more treasures. She's envious of the physical closeness of the lovers and prefers to leave them alone. The sands are silver white in the sun and the crystalline formation in the rocks glints and sparkles. She searches for tiny pieces to take back. She feels fit and can hardly believe her good fortune in being sent to such an exquisite area –

and for so many weeks. Eventually, she returns and spreads her finds out on the blanket.

'This time next week Dee, I wonder what you'll be doing,' Don says.

'That's a difficult one Don. I could be back in prison with a hopeless few years ahead of me. I like to imagine that I'll be at Mum and Dad's home with Thea and Maddy.'

'Don't think further ahead than the couple of days you'll have at Hattersley,' Elspeth advises. 'We'll be waiting anxiously up here for news.'

'It's nice to know that I'm leaving a couple of happy doctors to keep each other company.'

'No idea about company for yourself down in the Midlands,' Don enquires.

Dee makes a face at him. 'What chance have I had since I was put inside?'

'Two weeks in prison with all those women?'

She stares at him. What is he implying? She hasn't told Elspeth anything about those weeks in prison after the first mention, when she was in a rage on the night she arrived. Do Elspeth and Don need to know? They're both doctors and must be familiar with people from all walks of life. It might be a relief to tell them instead of keeping the two weeks bottled up inside.

'There was plenty of sex, if that's what you want to know, my cell mate was a predatory lesbian,' and she went on to tell them the whole story.

'Phew! That was enough to cope with in two weeks,' Don says when she's finished.

'Where was Jane in all this?' Elspeth asks, astonished at Dee's story. 'Didn't she know what was going on?'

'Frances was my prison visitor. I told her about Tracy and my fears. She taped the interview and left the cassette on the desk in the secretary's office. I overheard Jane tell Doctor Tupman that the jealous deputy governor Elvira Morgan, who didn't like me, had taken the tape out of the secretary's office and hidden it. Jane never received the information.'

'That did alter events,' Don says. If the fight hadn't happened, you would now be serving the last week of your remand sentence in prison, on the other hand, we would never have had the chance to meet you and you'd have missed getting to know us.'

'Tell me, does that mean that there were quite a number of lesbian prisoners, or women who needed sex and turned to each other? Did you find that objectionable?' Elspeth wanted to know.

How to answer that question?

'Erm...okay, I loved the sex.' Dee laughs. 'I was starved of sex.' She sees the lovers exchange understanding looks. 'But the situation nearly blew my mind.'

'Because it was sex with a woman?'

'Yes. It didn't take long to get used to the actual sex; Tracy was reputed to be the best lover in the wing.' She laughs again and they join in. 'It was sex being forced on me by a woman that I objected to. Sex with a woman you loved would be very different,' she says pensively, she's had time to think this through.

'It's the living with a woman openly that puzzles me. If homosexuality isn't even talked about in society, how does a heterosexual family behave toward a couple of men or women living next door? You must admit that Margaret and Frances, and Barry and Jim, belong to a privileged class. Hattersley is the ideal place in which to be private, – "the two eccentric women who live up at the Big House" kind of talk. Excuses are always made for wealthy people.'

'You're right,' Elspeth agrees, 'it is easier for some than others. There's a lot of prejudice and fear in the general public. I'll never understand how people can be so narrow minded and cruel to anyone who's different, or why people are upset by sexual activity. After all, it belongs to the private part of everyone's life. It only matters when it's harmful. I'm sure that nearly every child experiments erotically with same sex school friends, I know I did.'

'Me too,' Don adds and they laugh again. He lay down when the conversation started and Dee thought he was asleep. Elspeth prods him affectionately. Dee likes the way he keeps his arm round Elspeth with his hand lying lightly against her skirt.

'You asked me what I was dancing about that Saturday night. It wasn't just excitement because I'd peeked out of the window and seen the two of you kissing, I'd come to the important conclusion about myself that it doesn't matter whether I love a man or a woman. It's my responsibility and my business. I've been too afraid to open my mind to this possibility before. All I need now is someone to love,' she finishes ruefully.

'Right, so that answers my question,' Don says. 'You haven't got anyone for yourself down in the Midlands.'

Dee shades her eyes from the sun with her hand and watches some gulls wheeling over the water.

'Just between us,' she says hesitantly, 'I think I fell in love with Jane Pennyfields the first time I saw her. I thought I just admired her attractive appearance, her voice and the way she spoke to me, but I can't get her out of my mind. It's probably because I've had so much time on my hands and I've needed to pin my romantic dreams on someone. I'll recover when I'm back to looking after two children – or in another prison where the governor is not nice looking. Please don't mention that to the family Elspeth.

'I'll have to be careful as well, not to make the same mistake a second time, of putting the person I admire on a pedestal, like I did with Jon. I lost myself in trying to be worthy of him and felt increasingly inadequate when he showed interest in other women. I must be sure that I value the person I am before I commit to a relationship. There's a danger with a woman like Jane Pennyfields, not that she would be interested in me, whatever you think Elspeth,' Dee stops her before she can say anything. 'She's another very clever person like Jon and her authoritative manner thrills me. She's so confident. She wouldn't understand my uncertainties.'

'We are talking about the same Jane Pennyfields that rang her mother on Tuesday, breaking her heart because she felt so lonely in her position of authority; who said she wished her mother could love her in the same way she loved Julia?' Elspeth says quietly.

Dee is silenced.

'Don't forget young lady that I was around when Jane was born. I'm her very proud godmother. Yes, she's gorgeous looking but she's a sensitive, fine woman. You haven't misplaced your affection. She's worth a daydream or two. If I'd discovered that you were not a strong enough character to match Jane's personality I'd have discouraged you sharpish. As it is, should you both meet outside the prison walls I think you'd give her a good run for her money. And don't go talking about not being a valuable enough partner. I, Elspeth Hunter, declare you to be as well put together as a young woman of thirty-two can be.'

'So put that in your pipe and smoke it,' Don says lazily.

'Joking aside Don,' Elspeth shakes him, 'from the way Dee talks, and I know she's been mulling over these important issues, I thinks she's evolving a sensible approach to the whole issue. I'll be very interested to hear how you go on Dee.'

'In all seriousness so will I,' Don says. 'Now, shall we think about getting back?'

Romantic speculation is immediately replaced by reality. Two more days and she must leave.


## Tuesday 28th July

Elspeth and Dee are sitting in the parked Jeep at Thurso railway station by seven-forty five on Tuesday morning. They haven't talked much on the way there. It's not really an unhappy farewell for either of them. They know that they can communicate and if all goes well, they'll see each other again.

Greg arrives early and they hug with pleasure at their reunion. He quickly stows the picnic in the van, the hold-all with Dee's clothes, and the two precious carrier bags with treasures for Thea and Maddy.

'Dee was all right then Doctor was she? I was quite worried when I left her with you that day.'

'Oh, she was no end of trouble,' Elspeth claims. 'I'm glad to get rid of her.' But the way she embraces Dee and wishes her luck shows Greg that she's fibbing. 'I have to say Greg that she improved on acquaintance.'

'Thanks again for everything,' Dee whispers because the final leave-taking brings tears.

As Greg pulls away from the car-park, she sees Elspeth take a hanky out of her pocket and walk toward the Jeep wiping her eyes.

'She seems okay,' Greg remarks. 'I thought she was awfully stern the day I dropped you off.'

'It was a few weeks before we took to each other. I've tried to imagine what it must have been like for her to suddenly be asked to shelter an escaped prisoner. No wonder she was suspicious at first. I'm invited to come for a holiday with my children next year.'

'That'll be grand.'

'It will if I'm not in prison.'

'Aye well…there's that to deal with. Friday isn't it?'

'It's Friday.'

Dee sits back. She might as well enjoy the scenery. The grassy roadside verges are pink with sweeps of Rosebay Willow Herb and through the open window she catches whiffs of pungent Meadowsweet. The Rowan berries are turning to orange. Greg chats away.

'The tourist season's given my sister's Bed and Breakfast a good start. She's thrilled with the Staffordshire crocks.'

'Have you had a holiday?'

'I took the wife and kids on one of my delivery trips to Cornwall at the end of June. We stayed for a week in a caravan, near Falmouth. The weather was kind to us too.'

Travelling in the cab is a pleasure. The seat is high up and Dee can see over walls and hedges into fields and gardens. She can spy through the trees on wooded banks to where streams rush between the pebbles. It doesn't seem possible that she's in a world where there will be a Court Hearing on Friday. They stop for bacon rolls and the toilets. Then Greg makes a long run down, past Inverness, and doesn't stop until Perth where they both have a snooze.

'I've friends in Berwick upon Tweed,' Greg says. 'I don't get to see them often and they've asked us to stay the night. Is that okay with you?'

'What's our schedule for tomorrow?' Dee asks, nervous about any diversion.

'We'll set off early in the morning and take the scenic route through the Borders. You'll like that run. It'll take four to five hours, depending on how often we stop. We should get to Hattersley about two or three o'clock in the afternoon.'

Greg's friends have a shop in Castle Street. Greg and Dee arrive just after closing time. The kettle's on and they've mugs of tea in their hands almost before the introductions are over.

'What were you doing so far north Dee?' Jack, the husband asks.

Greg gives her an anxious look but she's ready for this question.

'I had a bit of an accident with a piece of furniture.' She shows them her scar. 'Greg and I have friends in common. They asked him to transport me to Scotland, where I've been staying with an old friend until the wound healed. I couldn't have gone to a lovelier place.'

'I'm not sure about that now,' Jack says, 'have you explored Northumberland at all?'

Dee shakes her head, relieved that her explanation satisfied him.

'Well, until you've seen some of our beaches you'd better not claim that the north coast of Scotland is the loveliest place.'

The evening meal introduces Dee to Scotch pies and vegetables, with syrup sponge and custard to follow. She's so full of food that the suggestion of a walk is welcome. Jack and his wife Elizabeth give her a run-down of Berwick's history. She'd no idea that the town is second only to Jerusalem in the number of times it's been invaded, England versus Scotland. Concentrating on information keeps her mind off the real reason she's in Berwick tonight.

They walk up on to the town walls and she's glad Elspeth packed the jumper because the breeze off the North Sea is chilly. The lighthouse winks at the end of the pier. Jack points out the shapes of Holy Island and Bamburgh Castle, looming shapes in the dusk. They shiver their way into a pub where Dee requests her favourite Guinness with a dash of lemonade, to the disgust of the landlord. She laughs because she always meets with that reaction.

'Murdering a good drink,' he says.

She could do without the word "murder" at the moment, though this is the town for it; hundreds of murders in years gone by. She's shown the hill that runs down to the River Tweed and the bridge that was completed in 1604 – with added information that the street ran red with blood! She doesn't refuse Elizabeth's offer of a hot water bottle at bedtime.

They're away early in the morning, stuffed again, this time with a full English breakfast. Dee moans and pats her tum.

'An English breakfast is the custom in the most northerly town in England,' Elizabeth says. 'I'm sure you've had plenty of porridge the other side of the border.'

'Thank you so much for making me welcome.'

Dee is near to tears again. She's grateful to all the kind people who've helped her to get through these three traumatic months. The anxiety is there in the pit of her stomach. In a few hours she'll be back, out of hiding. She's torn between wanting to be safe inside Hattersley and trying to slow up the return by staying longer at each stop. But Greg has a time-table.

Hawick is left behind, with its convenient large car-park and toilets. Sometimes the tree shaded road winds beside the river, at others it nestles between the folds of the hills. It's unbelievable on this sunny morning to conceive that in the three hundred years of Border warfare, men on horseback came killing and plundering in these outlying farmsteads.

The landscape flattens out. They pass the sign-post to Gretna Green. Longtown is left behind. They're back on the M6, travelling south. Even the high banks, white with Ox-eye daisies, can't gladden Dee's heart. Her safe retreat is hundreds of miles away. Her adventure is over.

## Thursday 30th July

Dee opens the restaurant door.

This is part of the daring venture planned by Margaret. She, Frances and Dee booked into the hotel after lunch and went shopping. Dee's name in the hotel register is Florence Gardner, a family name from her dad's side; Florence is a favourite aunty. Margaret is booked in as Taylor, Frances as Usher(using her mother's maiden name.) Margaret sweeps everyone along with her audacious ideas.

The hotel foyer is crowded, largely with men talking in loud voices. It's early and Dee has covered the distance from the lift door to the restaurant door without attracting attention, as far as she can tell. Not many of the tables in the dining room are occupied. The restaurant manager approaches her.

'I'd like to sit at that table for two by the window,' she says and he pulls out a chair, – 'no, I'd like to face the conservatory please, I'm dining alone. I'll be very happy to look at the plants while I eat. I'd like a glass of cream sherry please.'

The conservatory is huge, filled with ferns, broad leafed tropical plants and exotic flowers. This is all very luxurious, Dee's first time in a large hotel and she's feeling very pleased with her elegant appearance. She's wearing a simple black sheath dress, one of Margaret's necklaces and new shoes. Her hairstyle had grown out of shape but her hair is shiny and healthy. Barry has cut and dressed it. Her back is toward the diners so she shouldn't be detected and if she is, it will only mean one more night in custody, assuming that she's not pronounced guilty tomorrow.

The sherry charms her spirit and she listens to the pianist playing popular songs. *Stardust* she recognises and *For All We Know,* also *Somewhere My Love, I'm in the Mood for Love* and similar melodies. Conversation is hushed and the atmosphere romantic. She liked it when she and Jon ate at restaurants, before the girls were born, but it was always Chinese or Indian food, or lemon tea in tall glasses at the Kardomah. No music. She hears Margaret's voice, talking to Frances and steals a quick look behind. They're both making the best of the occasion by wearing their new dresses.

She enjoys her smoked salmon starter with a glass of white wine and has nearly finished eating the casseroled lamb course with a glass of red wine, when she freezes. She hears the unmistakable voice of The Penny, friendly and amused, speaking to someone as she passes behind Dee's chair. Dee glances over to the far end of the restaurant and sees with relief that The Penny is seated with her back toward her. The Penny's dinner date is an attractive blonde woman, tall and wearing a pretty summer dress. Dee turns in her chair slightly to make eye contact with Margaret and Frances. They grimace at each other, alarmed at the awkwardness of the situation.

Dee can't eat another morsel. The heart has gone out of her. She shouldn't be here. She's supposed to be in hiding. She's so conscious of being an escaped prisoner when she hears The Penny's voice that she might as well be dressed in a prison shirt and overalls – and here she's been sitting, her thoughts wallowing in romantic indulgence! She attracts the attention of the manager.

'I'd like to leave now. No, no thank you, no dessert or coffee. Is there another way out of the dining room, with access to the stairs?'

He takes her elbow and accompanies her to a side door. She makes her escape, avoiding the foyer.

She's crying with disappointment as she approaches her room. She can't see the lock and has to insert the key twice before she can successfully get it to turn. Once inside she lets the door bang shut behind her, kicks off her shoes and slides down into a disillusioned heap.

'I'm an idiot...so foolish,' she tells herself. 'I will persist with dangerous daydreams; imagining so intensely that I've made myself believe in possibilities. Now I'll have to undo all my hopes with regard to The Penny. I'm not going to blame myself. Anyone like me, who is emerging from a broken marriage needn't blame himself or herself for hoping that there would be a second chance, a relationship with a significant other that one could trust.' Hopefully she can rationalise the situation, talk some sense into herself.

'Why am I so hurt and disappointed? There's been Elspeth's teasing and my own hopes. Did I really fall in love with The Penny while pretending they were daydreams, despite my common sense and my self-cautioning about our different worlds? Did I just want someone on whom to fasten my affections while I was sad and lonely?' She can't answer her own questions.

'Tomorrow, if I'm set free there will be lots of love between the children and me and that is my life. They will compensate in part for personal loneliness. Housework, family and friends, if I've any left... will help me to sublimate.'

She drags herself up from the floor and undresses, carefully draping her finery on a hanger and hooking it over the wardrobe door, where she can admire it. Then she changes her mind. The dress belongs to the failure of the evening. She hangs it out of sight inside the wardrobe and puts on her nighty.

There's a knock on the door. Margaret calls to her. 'Dee, it's me, Margaret.' Dee opens the door and Margaret slips inside.

'Are you all right Dee? That was a close shave,' Margaret says. 'Jane didn't see you but her companion had seen your photo and thought she recognised you. She informed Jane and my zealous daughter shot over to our table. "Was it her?" she said. I didn't feel like being helpful so I said, "Good evening to you too dear." Jane was not amused.' They both giggle nervously. "Ask me nicely," I said to Jane and she more or less growled, "Was it Livesey?" I had to say, "Yes," – but I refused to let her know which room you were in. Frances and I made quite sure that they were still eating when we left the restaurant. You're safe for tonight.'

'I notice I'm still "Livesey" and a prisoner in Jane's eyes. Who was her dinner partner?'

'That was Annabel Priestley. Now, see if you can get some sleep. Goodnight dear.'

Seen her photo; was it the dreadful one in the newspaper or the snap that Elspeth took? If it was the latter, where was it on view so that Annabel Priestley could see it? The fact that Jane has kept her photo where it can be seen would have been food for delightful thought – not now.

Dee's hotel room is brown and well used. It's spacious and she pads about, laying out her clothes for the morning. From the fifth floor she can look out over the rooftops. She leaves the curtains undrawn and sits in bed, propped against a bank of pillows. Up here, there's a feeling of being pleasantly removed from the world. Tomorrow will bring her down to ground level. Hotel Reception will call her at seven.

# THE HEARING AND AFTERWARDS

Friday 31st July

She doesn't need the alarm call. After a disturbed night, she gets up at five o'clock to make a cup of tea. Sitting up in bed, she's able to watch the sun rise over the city skyline. She feels small and disconnected from the sound of voices and the increasing noise of traffic as the city comes to life. This is all ridiculous, her mum's favourite word. How absurd that shortly she must walk along the street and make herself known at the courthouse. Prisoners should arrive under escort, in handcuffs. This way she will avoid publicity, the photographers and journalists that hound prisoners for statements on their way to and from court. She'll be glad when she's safely inside the building. Her eyes fill with tears. She'll see her mum. Margaret, Frances and Barry will be there and Jon. Jim was hoping to alter his shift so that he could come.

She boils the kettle and empties a second sachet of coffee into her cup. There's a knock on the door and her light breakfast order arrives. She enjoys the fruit, stewed green figs and eats the boiled egg with a sliver of buttered toast. She doesn't know when her next meal will be or where she'll be eating it.

She stands by the window, taking comfort from the warm cup of coffee in her hands and stares out bleakly at the scene. Twelve weeks! Twelve weeks and she's no idea what the outcome of this morning will be. If she'd stayed in prison there would have been lawyers' visits and possibly barristers' and she would have been told how her case was progressing. Talk about going out there cold! She's a pawn in a game over which she has no control.

Eight-fifteen; they agreed that eight-fifteen would give her time to reach the courthouse. She walks out of the hotel foyer wearing Jane's check shirt and stone coloured slacks. She feels better once she's on the move. By eight-thirty she's at the bottom of the courthouse steps. She stops for a moment, surprised. There's a crowd of photographers and journalists hanging about on the pavement and a buzz of excitement. Is it to do with her? She climbs the steps and speaks quietly to the policeman on duty.

'I'm Deanna Livesey. My Hearing is scheduled for this morning. Can you take me to wherever I'm supposed to be please?' There, that hadn't been too difficult.

If the policeman is shocked he doesn't show it. He raises an arm and waves it as though to catch attention. Dee spins round to see why, and then realises that he's pointing her out to the crowd at the bottom of the steps. A few hectic minutes follow, in which photographers run and shout and cameras flash.

'Where've you been Mrs Livesey?' she hears and, 'How'd you do your disappearing act Deanna?' 'Can we have your story Deanna?' The policeman takes her arm and ushers her inside.

'Sorry about that,' he says. 'Your case has been fairly dramatic. I couldn't spoil their fun.'

Half an hour later, she's sitting in a holding cell, handcuffed to a policewoman.

The Penny comes in. Dee's gut contracts at the sight of The Penny's smart uniformed figure but after the disappointment of last night, she's not embarrassed.

'Good morning Miss Pennyfields. We meet again in less than pleasant circumstances.' She offers her left hand for The Penny to shake.

The Penny holds on to Dee's hand and looks at her watch. 'Officer, we're not due in court for another ten minutes. I'd like a word alone with Mrs Livesey please.'

'I was told to stay handcuffed to her.'

The Penny lets go of Dee's hand and shrugs her shoulders.

'You do know Miss Pennyfields is the governor of Stonebridge Women's Prison,' Dee says to the officer. 'She's not likely to abduct me. She's probably going to tell me off for all the trouble I've caused her.'

'Sorry Mrs Livesey, I can't take the cuffs off.'

The fear and desperation are back, those lovely weeks of freedom and now the renewed threat of a prison sentence. 'I want to ask you something Miss Pennyfields. Do you know where I'll be sent if I'm found guilty?'

'Let's hope that won't be the verdict but, if you are found guilty, you will be transferred out of Stonebridge; not that you've spent much time *in* that establishment.' She smiles encouragingly. 'Let's hope the verdict will be favourable. Judge Howell is in charge of the proceedings this morning. He's fair.'

'Judge Howell! He's a friend of a far-distant friend.'

'I know.'

Dee's name is called. Her case is the first to be heard. Entering the packed courtroom takes all her courage. She sees her mum in the visitors' gallery, with the Hattersley crowd. Good, they've met each other. Jon is there too and acknowledges her with a wave. The Penny is at the front with lawyers and officials. The policewoman and Dee sit side by side in the dock; they have no option.

'Please be upstanding.'

The Hearing is underway.

Judge Howell arranges his bundle of documents on the bench and moves his drinking glass and water to within reach. He adjusts his half moon spectacles. Dee looks at him with interest. This is Elspeth's friend and soon he'll be sleeping in the bed she's recently vacated. He scans the room full of people and brings his gaze to rest on Dee. She could almost believe the interest to be mutual. He clears his throat and says, 'Hm.'

'In any case that comes before a court it is evidence, *evidence*,' he repeats with emphasis, 'that decides the fate of the person on trial. My learned associates and I,' he gestures towards the legal presences, 'have spent time in consultation prior to this Hearing. We have discussed the matter of evidence relating to this case. Our decision has been reached and I will now present it to you.

'Deanna Livesey is accused of murdering her mother-in-law, Madeleine Theresa Livesey, on Tuesday 5th May this year. Evidence presented by the arresting officer,' he indicates the detective sitting in the front of the courtroom, 'was sufficiently damning for the accused to be remanded in custody for a period of three months.'

He peers at the prisoner over his glasses.

'I hear that Deanna Livesey has served the greater part of her remand sentence in far flung parts of the British Isles, or should I say convalesced? According to my information she was injured in the second week of her detention, abducted in the third, and Her Majesty has been denied her presence at Stonebridge Women's Prison for the remaining period of nine weeks. I hear also, that she made a valiant attempt to return to custody and that a combination of weakness and nervous illness prevented the success of her plan.'

How does he know that? Dee stares at him with open mouthed astonishment. He turns his attention to the court.

'I have listened to the tapes recorded during interviews with prisoner Deanna Livesey. I've read all the correspondence written by her to her family and friends. I have here,' he holds up a sheaf of papers, 'letters written protesting her innocence. Salutary though this information might be it lacks convincing evidence to prove that Deanna Livesey is not guilty of the crime of which she is accused.' There's a dramatic pause in which Judge Howell pours a glass of water and drinks a mouthful. 'However,' he begins, 'however...it appears that she has a perceptive friend on the northernmost shores of our isles.'

Dee hasn't recovered from listening incredulously to the news that every word she's written has been read, every word she's spoken at interview has been examined, and now this mention of Elspeth!

Judge Howell holds up a piece of paper and everyone in the room can see that it's a pencil sketch. 'A person who must be nameless, who has been caring for the prisoner at her home for the past eight and a half weeks, sent me this piece of paper with the drawing that you can all see. During an evening of, what I can only call domestic dimensional comparisons, this drawing was completed by the accused.'

Dee is given another penetrating look. She feels as though this friend of Elspeth's is dangling her like a fish on the end of a line.

'The drawing was posted to me by the nameless person as soon as she heard that it had fallen to my lot to preside at this morning's proceedings. What do we see on this piece of paper?'

He hands the sheet to an official who projects the drawing on to a screen for the public to view. Dee is horrified! Her roughly drawn, disproportionate sketch is displayed on a screen for all to see. Crafty Elspeth! That evening was fun. Had Elspeth steered the conversation, directed their activity to this end? Judge Howell continues.

'You see here a bed, television, armchair, table, chest of drawers, bookcase and a pine coffee-table situated under the window. Can we see a projection of the police photograph of the scene, taken on the morning of the arrest please?

'You will observe that the photograph shows a different arrangement of furniture in the room. Mrs Cairns, the prisoner's cleaning lady, started to prepare the room for the arrival of the prisoner's mother, Mrs Warburton, who was expected for a visit on the day of the arrest. In fact, Mrs Cairns went home shortly after her employer had been arrested, as did Mrs Warburton, – the latter taking with her the younger Livesey child, Madeleine. The room was not slept in. Observe that in the photograph the bed has been re-positioned and the coffee-table removed from under the window.

'On the morning of May 7th, detectives lifted fingerprints from the sides of the window-frame in the room. They revealed that Madeleine Livesey senior had placed her hands there. It was conceived that she could not, at the age of eighty-six have stepped up on to the window-sill and therefore must have been pushed to her death by her daughter-in-law. Had Madeleine Livesey leant over the sill and let herself fall to her death, there would not have been fingerprints in those positions on the frame.'

Dee feels as though the colour is draining out of her face. She mustn't faint.

'Exhibit one alters the whole picture. It is a representation of Madeleine Livesey's bed-sit on the night of 5th May, the arrangement of furniture as it existed before Mrs Cairns began her cleaning and rearranging. Detectives re-visited the Livesey home immediately after this drawing arrived last week. The bed-sit has remained undisturbed since 7th May and the prisoner's arrest.

'What the prisoner did not include in her sketch, was a circular, plastic lace mat in the centre of the coffee-table.' He gestures to the official to hold up the article. 'The officers dusted the coffee-table for prints and when they lifted the lace mat, there underneath was a perfect imprint of a size six ladies' slipper, Madeleine Livesey's slipper. This is the evidence we needed.'

His eyes travel round the hushed courtroom.

'We can now state that, the fingerprints on the window frame were made by Madeleine Livesey when she climbed on to the coffee-table, prior to throwing herself out of the window.'

There are gasps of astonishment all over the room and outbursts of chatter. Dee's eyes prick with unshed tears. She has a vision of the poor woman, standing on the coffee-table with the window open, dusk outside, crazed and intent on throwing herself into the space below. Judge Howell looks over his glasses and waits until the people settle down.

'This evidence proves, without a shadow of doubt, that Deanna Livesey is not guilty of the murder of her mother-in-law.'

There's another burst of noise and some cheers. She suspects Barry and Jim, if he's arrived. Judge Howell looks reprovingly over his spectacles and the courtroom falls silent.

'Nothing excuses the haste of the arrest or the neglect of the before and after scenes. Had Deanna Livesey not been pressed by numerous demands for her attention on the day of the arrest, she would probably have entered the room with the detectives and noticed the re-arrangement of the furniture. Whether that would have meant anything to her it's not possible to say. Mrs Cairns had carried out her instructions. He held up a scrap of paper and read, "Can you clean Grandma Livesey's room and make it look a bit different, ready for Mum?" Unfortunately,' he says, looking directly at Dee, 'your concern for your mother's welfare made you issue instructions that helped to precipitate the trauma of the last three months.'

She's partly responsible because of one little sentence!

'This is a sorry story of a wretched elderly person attempting to take her own life and the resounding effect it has had on the young woman seated before me. Deanna Livesey is to be pitied for the suffering and indignity caused by a wrongful accusation.

'There is the matter of the law being broken by Deanna Livesey's abduction from hospital, an event to which she acquiesced and in which she played an active part.' He picks up a folder and opens it, referring to the contents of the first page.

'These are her hospital records. They indicate that, on the morning of the kidnap she was in a state of nervous shock, under sedation, and in considerable pain from the injuries she sustained in prison. I am advised by medical authorities that she was in a condition of diminished responsibility.' He takes a second page.

'This letter informs me that on Thursday 11th June, Deanna Livesey walked eight miles in an attempt to reach a distant telephone box, from which she intended to phone the police; distant enough to avoid incriminating her hostess, or guardian.' He closes the folder and puts it to one side.

'The proof of Deanna Livesey's innocence, plus her valiant attempt to make amends for the illegality of her situation, would appear to have redressed her wrongful remand sentence. Deanna Livesey, you are hereby exonerated from serving further time at Her Majesty's pleasure.'

More cheers and chatter in the courtroom. This is the news Dee has hoped for. Until today, her pathetic attempt to return to prison has made her squirm. This morning she's commended for it! Judge Howell holds up his hand for silence.

'We move on to the abduction from hospital, the kidnap that removed a prisoner from custody, albeit from a medical facility. I have to report that, despite extensive enquiries on the part of the police, the persons responsible for this crime have not been discovered. The seriousness of the action, although it cannot be dismissed, is somewhat mitigated by the fact that we assume it was carried out by well meaning perpetrators. We have seen that they removed the prisoner from one form of custody to another, one in which they knew she would be cared for and restored to health. In the light of Deanna Livesey's innocence there is a strange sort of justice at work here and nothing further needs to be said about the matter...at this time.'

His eyes sweep the room and seem to hesitate on the row of seats occupied by the Pennyfields family.

'Deanna Livesey, I hope that you will be able to resume your life, remembering some of the good things that have resulted from the last three months, and leaving behind the unfavourable ones. This case is discontinued.'

The assembly stands as the judge returns to his chambers.

In the last few minutes Dee has vacillated between fear and hopes of freedom. She's dazed. What happens now? She doesn't know what to do. She has no money. Her mum's here. Does her mum know that she wants to go home with her and will she let her stay for a few days? She can't face her own home yet. She just wants to be with Thea and Maddy.

Jon pushes through the people in front of her and takes her arm for support. He steers a passage out of the courtroom door to a bench in the corridor. Dee sits down heavily.

'I'm glad that's all over Dee,' he says sympathetically. 'It's been a rotten time for you. Thea's at your mother's. Let me know when you want to come home. I think we both know that the sooner I move out the better. I'll arrange for my stuff to be taken out of the house. Put this in your pocket, its Sarah's name, address and telephone number, that's where I'll be. I hope you recover from this ordeal soon. Thea's longing to see you. She's put on a brave face during the whole time you've been gone, but she's missed you terribly. We did our best but we're not you.' He smiles and squeezes her hand. 'I'll get off now – hope everything goes okay.'

There's stir and bustle all round Dee. Her husband's gone, leaving her with a contact number for another woman's home.

She has no "old life" to return to. There's a divorce to negotiate. Does she say goodbye to these new friends who have been so kind and generous? She feels panic rising and buries her face in her hands, whimpering with fear.

She hears Frances say, 'Dee needs help.'

Her mum is there, her hand on her arm. 'It's all right Dee,' she says and draws her hands away from her face. She wipes her tears with her hanky and winces when she sees the ugly scar above her eyebrow. Dee sits limply. The next thing she hears is Margaret's command.

'Head down Dee,' and once again she's bending forward from the seat of her chair, this time with Margaret's hand on her back.

When she comes to, she sees Jane and her mother talking. Barry hands her a cup of sweetened tea which she sips thankfully.

'Chop, chop,' Barry says. 'I've ordered your coffees.' He shunts their group in the direction of the café.

'Barry,' his sister calls out to him, 'I suggest that we all have lunch at The Lion's Head Hotel. Will it be convenient for you and Jim to do the honours to the railway station after lunch, for Mrs Warburton and Dee please? I have to get back to work.'

Dee wants to giggle when she sees Barry do one of his exaggerated bows before he takes her mum's arm and they head for the café.

'Deanna, will you come with me if you're feeling better and we'll finalize the court proceedings,' The Penny says.

The necessary forms are signed. Dee is handed the little bundle of her possessions. The clothes she will not want to wear again or the wedding ring. The clothes she stands up in, and her finery from last night, are all she has to take with her to her mum and dad's. She'll miss The Penny's good quality wardrobe. The Penny puts her hand under Dee's elbow as they leave the courthouse by the door that leads to the car-park. Dee is very conscious of the touch and wants to discourage any familiarity between them. The Penny is a prison governor and she's a newly released prisoner. She moves her bag of possessions so that it's between them. The Penny lets go of her arm.

'Will the reporters have gone? I'd rather not be quizzed by them,' Dee asks nervously.

'The advantage of leaving the premises by the back door, in the company of the governor of Stonebridge Prison, is that you'll be spared the nuisance,' The Penny says confidently.

Dee breathes a sigh of relief; she can hardly believe that it's all over. She looks up at the sun, shining on the leaves and well formed conkers in the huge chestnut tree by the car-park and feels her spirit lift.

'I must ring Elspeth. I promised to let her know the outcome of the Hearing,' she says

'You can phone from the pub.'

The Penny opens the car door for her. It's delightful to sink onto the leather seat and stretch out her legs, just as comfortable as she imagined it would be.

'Do you think we could drop the formalities now you're a free woman?' The Penny asks. 'My name is Jane.'

'I like to be called Dee. How do you do Jane?'

The laugh that greets her introduction is as rich and delightful as Dee would have expected. 'I do very well thank you,' Jane says and looks intently at her companion.


Their lunch party is not dull. Dee makes sure that she's not sitting next to Jane. The sooner she's away from her presence, the sooner she can focus on the days ahead. She must keep her mind off dreams and on reality. Barry relates the details of her escape in whispered colourful terms. Heads bend over the table to catch his words. The story is all the more exciting told in hushed tones.

'I'm relieved that it's all over,' Margaret says quietly, 'fortunately we've escaped detection. Fear that the involvement of my family might be discovered, has been hanging over me like a black cloud.'

'I couldn't imagine how the escape had been carried out,' Dee's Mum says. 'Your phone calls Margaret, even though we didn't know who you were, came as a tremendous relief. It seems you were ridiculously brave all of you. Dee can fill me in on the rest of the story.'

Poor Elspeth; she has quite a job to sort out the day's events. Margaret and Dee take it in turns to speak into the receiver and Dee's Mum wants to thank Elspeth for taking good care of her daughter. The main news is clear, Dee has been pronounced free from suspicion of murder and Elspeth is delighted.


Dee and her mum lean back, exhausted, in their seats in the railway carriage. The farewells at the railway station were brief because they had to hurry to catch the train. Margaret remembered the bags of treasures for the girls. Dee looks across at her mum, who has once again fulfilled her uncomplaining, supportive mother-role, and her eyes fill with tears. They sat like this when she was seven and came out of hospital after her tonsil operation. She cried then, and her mum asked the gentleman next to her if he would change seats so that her daughter could sit on her knee. She smiles at her mum through her tears; she's too big to sit on her knee now.

The porter at Burylane makes a show of opening the carriage door and sees them safely on to the platform. 'Mrs Warburton, Dee,' he says and touches his cap.

Dee's mother carries the hold-all and takes her arm. She seems to know that Dee needs her support. They walk the quarter of a mile from the station and Dee is surprised to see how many villagers are standing at their garden gates as they pass.

'Mrs Warburton, Dee,' they say. 'Good to see you again Dee.' 'Glad it's all over Dee.' 'Mrs Warburton.' 'Welcome home Dee.'

She hadn't expected this. She gets some sense of how awful her imprisonment has been for everybody and she's ashamed. She thought only of herself during those three months. Her smile is bleak and her mum holds her arm tightly. They stand still outside her Mum and Dad's house so that she can collect herself before she meets Thea and Maddy. Dad, a retired railway man, has been listening out for the train and waiting.

'It was on the one o'clock news,' he says in a strangled voice and hugs her. 'The girls are watching children's television in the front room.'

The girls take a few moments before they realise she's there and then she's nearly bowled over by two figures hurtling across the room. The three of them fall on to the settee in a heap of love and kisses. Maddy perches on her knee.

'Did you bring us a present Mum?'

'I went out on to the beach every day and looked for pretty shells and stones for you. The lady I was staying with is called Elspeth. She would like us to go for a holiday next year and then you can play on the lovely beach and gather your own shells. There's one collection for you Maddy and one for Thea. You could spread them out on Granddad's patio.'

She's off. Life has returned to normal for Maddy, not for Thea. She hasn't let go of Dee's hand since they sat down. Dee pulls her on to her knee and she bursts into tears.

'I didn't like it Mummy, I didn't like it. I wanted you all the time. I didn't tell Daddy. I waited until he'd gone downstairs and then I cried under the covers. We went to Sarah's at the weekends and Daddy and Sarah slept in the same bed and I didn't like it Mummy. They were always kissing and I tried not to look. I knew you wouldn't like it Mummy.'

They hang on to each other. Perhaps she should have told Thea about Sarah and Jon. She confesses she hadn't known what to do.

'That was a big shock for you to be left alone with someone you didn't know,' she says when Thea is calmer. 'I'm so sorry. I did know about Daddy and Sarah. I wasn't sure how to tell you and then I was taken away and I'd left it too late.

'Your daddy and I haven't been in love for quite a long time now. I've been very sad about it but as long as you and Maddy are happy to live with me we'll be okay. Daddy will keep in touch with you. He'll always be your daddy.

'Will we live in our house?'

'We'll have to move to a smaller house so that I can afford to pay for it. I'll probably be a teacher again and earn the money to keep us.'

'I'll go and look at my present now,' she says and Dee breathes more easily. Her mum has been listening and their eyes meet. Things are as okay as they can be.


Her Mum has a rest while Dee watches the girls play in the bath at bedtime. Maddy insists on her favourite ritual once she's wrapped in a towel, *Rock a bye baby on the treetop,* and screams when Dee pretends to let her fall.

Once they're tucked in bed, Dad takes over with his singing lessons. Dee squats on the top stair and listens. Dad is the adjudicator and comments on their individual rendering of a nursery rhyme. Then he marks them out of ten for diction and breathing etc. The competition between the two girls is furious and very amusing.

'Your turn now,' Dad says to Dee and she reads the bedtime stories.

'This is a different story book,' she says.

'Sarah gave it to me. She has lots of books for children because she teaches students how to be teachers, like Daddy.'

Dee is relieved that Thea can talk about the Jon and Sarah situation. At last the girls settle down and Dee joins her mum and dad in the sitting room. It's all so normal. The past three months are beginning to take on a dream-like quality.

'How are you feeling Dee?' her dad asks.

'I feel well Dad, if that's what you mean. I hardly dare believe that it's all over. Now I'm back here the whole episode seems like a fairy-tale. I'm the equivalent of Cinderella; Grandma Livesey's the witch who stirred up all the trouble and the detective might have been her 'familiar spirit,' – he was so keen to fight her corner and prove me guilty. The prison was the castle in the story and there were plenty of witches inside! Margaret's the Good Fairy and lives in a lovely mansion. Her family and friends do her bidding when she waves her magic wand.'

'No Prince Charming in your fairy-tale?'

'There was a Princess Charming, – wouldn't you agree Mum that the prison governor is charming?'

'She's a very handsome woman.' Her mum hesitates. 'Dee, I couldn't help noticing, but I'm not sure if I was imagining things, are Margaret and her friend Frances…together?'

'Yes, they are.'

'And the son Barry and his friend Jim?'

'Yes.'

'Isn't that unusual in a family?'

'I can't say Mum. They're the first openly homosexual couples I've met. Up to now I've only suspected that some couples might be homosexual. Julia, the daughter that died had boyfriends, but I think Jane Pennyfields might prefer women, from what I've heard.' She decides to take this opportunity to enlarge on the topic. 'Some of the women in prison were like that and made life difficult, one in particular, the one sharing my cell. She's a lesbian and I…well, shall we say, she wouldn't leave me alone.'

'Oh Dee, that must have been awful for you!'

'Not really Mum. The fact that she threatened me with trouble if I didn't comply was awful. The rest was just sex, and we all know what that's about. Jon has played away for so long that I didn't altogether object to the sex.'

'You're not saying that you're a lesbian are you?' Her dad sounds worried.

'I don't know Dad. If the Pennyfields are anything to go by, I can't see that, apart from the fact that they sleep together, lesbians are any different from other women. I definitely think it's possible to fall in love with someone of the same sex.'

'You were always in love with one teacher or another at Grammar School.'

'I was Mum. I don't know how you put up with my frequent crushes.' At this stage she daren't get any nearer to admitting that she fell in love with Jane Pennyfields.

'Well, I'm glad that family was good to you and I'm sure they're all very nice people,' Dad says. 'I can't say that I would be comfortable in their company. I've never liked that sort of thing. I'll go and shut the windows in the greenhouse.'

That will do for a start, it's the first time they've mentioned the subject seriously. Dee is ready for bed. She doesn't tell her mum and dad that she's longing for bedtime because she loves everything about Hattersley and wants to be on her own to think about its occupants. She loves Elspeth and Don. She's hyped on excitement and needs to go over today and everything that was said. She wants to ache for her disappointed love for Jane, to at least keep feeling, until she can let the memories fade.


## Saturday 1st August

Saturday begins with chanting "White rabbits, white rabbits, white rabbits," making wishes, and hoping for happy school holidays and good weather. It's a child orientated day to everyone's satisfaction.

Dee wears one of her mum's dresses while the check shirt and stone coloured trousers are washed – again. She will have to go home to get a change of clothes.


## Sunday 2nd August

In the morning there's a debate, as to whether the girls will go to chapel with their granny or stay at home with their mum, when a bright red sports' car draws up outside the house.

'Hi Dee,' Barry calls from the driving seat. 'I see I got here before the others.'

The others! Who's coming? Yesterday helped her to adjust to the life she knows. If the Pennyfields family comes, their two separate worlds will join up and she'll be confused. They were her rescuers. What is her relation to them now? They never said anything about keeping in contact and will The Penny be one of "the others"?

A curious Thea and Maddy look up at the tall young man, immaculately dressed, in a lightweight lemon coloured sweater and grey slacks.

'Introduce me Dee.' He solemnly shakes their hands.

'I like your car,' Maddy pipes up. 'Can I have a ride in it please?'

'You can indeed, but not at this very minute. There's your granddad and I haven't been introduced to him.'

'Dad, this is Barry Pennyfields.'

Introductions over, Barry is quick to notice Dad's roses.

'Mr Warburton, this *Deep Secret* rose has wonderful blooms, knocks spots off mine this year. It is *Deep Secret* isn't it? Darker than *Josephine Bruce* and,' he bends to smell the rose, – 'oh the fragrance!'

Dee can see that her dad is impressed with Barry's appearance and manners but will he be able to overcome his prejudice about gay men? It's a promising sign that Barry is invited to see the roses in the back garden. He disappears with a child attached to each hand.

She and her mum wait in the drive to greet the occupants of the Daimler that parks behind Barry's car. Good, she can cope with Margaret and Frances. Frances has a quiet stability that she finds comforting and she wears Liberty fabric blouses. Margaret is lively and challenging. The conversation's never dull if Margaret's around, nor is one quite sure what she'll say or do next. But they fade into the background when Dee sees the rear door of the Daimler open and The Penny ease her long legs out of the back of the car. She loses her steadiness of purpose immediately. She doesn't know how to behave. She just hopes that her dithery state is not outwardly visible.

The newcomers are taken round to the back garden to meet her Dad. Thea and Maddy make a point of introducing themselves. Dee goes into the house to help her mum make coffee.

'Well I must say Dee, you and Jane look like twins.' Margaret comments when they're settled on the patio chairs.

'I haven't got any of my own clothes here,' Dee explains. 'I wore some of Mum's and washed and ironed these yesterday.'

'When I saw you wearing my favourite shirt in court on Friday,' Jane says, 'I went straight out and bought myself a new one. I wondered why I couldn't find that shirt in my wardrobe. I suppose it's been to Scotland and back.'

'It's my favourite too. Can I keep it please?'

'You don't think I want it back after you've been wearing it all these weeks!' Everybody laughs and one of Dee's questions is answered. Jane has a sense of humour.

'Mr and Mrs Warburton,' Margaret says, 'we particularly want to visit Blake's Nursery. Their fame as rose specialists has reached our part of the world and Barry would never forgive us if we didn't have a look round.'

'It will be a pleasure to show you the nursery,' Dad says. 'We've watched the business grow over the years. Mr Blake began with one strip of land, not far from our house, and now he has fields of roses.'

'Would everybody like to go out to lunch afterwards? We'd like to take us all out for a treat. Is The Greyhound Hotel that we passed on the way here a good place for Sunday lunch?'

Dad and Mum have heard that it is. They rarely go out for meals. The party makes ready for departure and walks toward the cars. Jane has wandered off to look at the pool.

'Aren't you coming Jane?' Margaret asks.

'I've done my whack with gardens this year; running around, trying to impress a certain prisoner was quite enough thank you. You go off and leave me to catch up with Dee, unless you want to go too Dee?'

Dee shakes her head. 'I'd rather not go. It's too soon to mix with people who know me. I don't want to talk about what's happened.' The real reason she keeps to herself.

'Mr Warburton, is The Greyhound within walking distance?' Jane asks.

'Your quickest way is the path across the field. Dee knows the way.'

Jane and Dee sit on the garden swing. Jane tucks one of her legs underneath her and sits sideways facing Dee. Dee has folded her arms, she feels vulnerable and needs to keep a barrier between them.

'We'd better start at the beginning Dee,' Jane says. 'I'm really sorry about the violence at the prison and your injuries. I met Annabel Priestley for the first time on the day Frances visited you and stayed to have tea with her. If I'd gone straight back to Stonebridge I'd have seen the tape before Elvira Morgan could remove it from Joan's office.'

Three months since Jane and Annabel Priestley met and they've been going to concerts together and dining out; not the information Dee wants to hear.

'The tape made quite interesting listening, I have to add.'

Dee glances at her. She's smiling mischievously. This is definitely another side to the non-communicative prison governor. She suddenly remembers all the stuff about Tracy Manners on the tape, about enjoying sex with her, about wanting The Penny to think of her as a person and saying that she thought she was gorgeous.

'Annabel recognised you when you were leaving the restaurant last Thursday. I didn't like to turn round and stare and by the time I got to my feet you'd gone.'

'Annabel Priestley's never seen me.'

'Oh yes she has. The photo Elspeth sent? I've got it pinned on the notice board in my flat.'

So, Annabel Priestley goes to Jane's flat. More unwelcome news.

'What would you have done if you'd seen me?'

'Don't ask... I'm glad I didn't see you.'

'So my photo merits a drawing pin on the kitchen notice board, not a frame in the lounge?' Dee's recovering her confidence and pleasure in Jane's company.

'Don't push it! Photos can be torn up. It was risky of Mum to keep it and even more foolish of me to put it on display. Anyway, why are you sitting with your arms folded in that uptight way? Don't you know I'm an old hand at body language? I know damn well you're mad at me. If it makes you any happier to know, it was Annabel who asked me to dine with her last Thursday, not the other way round. She's in the throes of a budding relationship with a woman called Deirdre and it isn't going smoothly. You thought I was seeing Annabel didn't you? Go on Dee, admit it.

You thought she was my date. You've been cool with me ever since Thursday.'

Dee looks down at her folded arms and tries to hide a smile.

'Honestly Dee, you're like a petulant child. Unfold your arms and look at me. It's no use pretending you don't like me because I have it on good authority that you do.'

That means Elspeth has told her, no one else knows.

'I asked Elspeth not to tell you.'

'Ah, but did you make her promise not to tell me?'

'Would it have made any difference?'

'Probably not, – anyway I was glad of the information. I wanted to know where I stood with you. I'll let you in on a secret. I wasn't going to wear this shirt today. I fancied myself in a blue cotton stretch top but then I remembered you'd learnt "lesson one" and I didn't want my breasts to give you too much temptation.'

Dee shouts with laughter at this. She was listening that day!

'That's better. Now unfold your arms and look at me.'

'I can't look at you Jane. I'd give away everything I feel, and it would be embarrassing.'

'Don't you want to see what I feel?' she whispers. 'I fell in love with you the day I interviewed you. Didn't you wonder why I stood rooted to the spot? The feeling was so powerful that I couldn't speak or move after you'd struggled to explain yourself. If I'd taken a step toward you, I'd have taken you in my arms, sad, plucky prisoner that you were. My position as Governor is absolutely clear with regard to personal contact with prisoners so I couldn't do anything about it. I tried to see you every day.'

'You called me pestiferous.'

'Well, weren't you just, – flirting with me and dancing round the rake!'

'I waited till you'd gone before I danced round the rake.'

'That's what you thought. I know all the vantage points at Stonebridge.'

'What about the beastly dressing down you gave me re privilege and then taking me off the garden job?'

'That's the other apology I want to make. Did you have any idea why I reacted like that?' Dee shakes her head. 'I was jealous! You were laughing and talking with Mary Burns and you disappeared into the shed with her. I couldn't bear the thought that the two of you might be making love. I ordered you to work in the laundry because I wouldn't have to see you every day. Dee, can we go inside? I need to pay a call and we're altogether too visible to your curious next door neighbour.'

Dee shows Jane the downstairs cloakroom and runs upstairs to the bathroom. She nips into her bedroom to run a comb through her hair and sees Jane reflected in her dressing table mirror. She's come upstairs and is standing in the doorway.

'The toilet was an excuse to get you out of the public eye.'

They meet in the middle of the room, like magnets drawn together by powerful attraction. Dee's erogenous zone is unlocked by their first kiss as surely as if Jane turned a key. She's not sure if her legs will keep her upright.

'Get your kit off,' Jane orders.

Dee's head jerks back in surprise – this is not what she expected to hear but she co-operates in the removal of shirts and bras.

'I've got you to myself at last, hot ass – time for rumpie-pumpie,' Dee is astonished to hear Jane say.

'You found a dictionary of slang!'

Jane ignores the suggestion. 'I'm hot for you doll, get it on with me.'

Dee wants to laugh but Jane is unsmiling and seriously into nuzzling breasts. 'I suppose you wanna get into my knickers?' she says, connecting with her lover's playful mood.

'Sure do bitch.' They unzip pants, kick them out of the way, step out of briefs and arrive in a heap on the bed.

'I'm ready lover,' Dee says but she can't help smiling.

'I see you're ready for the horizontal mambo,' Jane says and pins her to the bed. 'Some prisoners are more trouble than others but I'm on to you babe.'

'Okay you've got me honey, now let me grope your pussy.'

And then they roll away from each other, laughing hysterically. The more they try to stop the more they give vent to shrieks. Dee wonders what the neighbours will think. 'Now look what we've done,' she says when they've recovered. 'We've de-fused our passion, and horizontal mambo notwithstanding, I was ready to give you my all.'

'Don't set me off. We haven't got time to make love. The laugh did us good after all that tension.' Jane leans over Dee and plays with her nipples. 'I went straight out and bought a dictionary of slang after your interview. It wouldn't have been the "done thing" for prisoners to see me browsing through the prison library copy. I've listened to that sort of talk for years and never repeated a word of it. Talking dirty doesn't come naturally, so I won't make a habit of it, but I like using the word fuck in its right context. I knew what you were talking about when you said the prisoners were trying to shock you. As a deputy, I was more in contact with them and they did the same to me.'

'Didn't you and Monica talk dirty?'

'How do you know about Monica?'

'I pretended to be asleep in a hospital bed.'

'Deceitful wretch! No, she was my first affair. It was passionate rather than playful. We fell for each other at a party when we were both alcoholically enhanced. I think she found me sexually tame. It didn't take her long to move on to someone else. What about you and Tracy Manners?'

'She was persuasive and intense.'

'Did you fall for her?'

'No, she was frightening. After the initial shock of being forced into sex, I was grateful for the experience, but she made my life miserable with her bullying.'

'She's had her "comeuppance". She's toeing the line now and hoping for early release. Did you fall for Mary Burns?'

'No, but I'd like to keep in touch with her. She's a nice woman, great company, and she's going to need friends when she gets out. I'm afraid that once my heart was lost to a prison governor, I had no interest in any of the women.'

That statement earns Dee more kisses. Jane lies down beside her.

'Mum guessed I'd fallen for you. She has eagle perception where Barry and I are concerned and she wasn't happy. That's why she wheedled her way into the hospital with Frances to give you the once over. She reckons she had a twofold reason for rescuing you, one because of Julia and the other because of me. It was a good job she arranged your rescue before you were totally cracked up, though I could have killed her at the time.' She looks at her watch. 'I suppose we'd better set off to meet the others. Are you disappointed because we didn't make love?'

'It's bliss being in love and taking time to get to know you. I'm delighted that you're such fun. When I got no verbal response from you at the prison I thought you might not be into small talk. Is it forward of me to hope that we'll indulge in sex before long?'

'It's a foregone conclusion.'

Barry opens the front door. 'You guys coming? Where are you?'

'We're up here Barry,' Jane calls. He bounds up the stairs.

'Come on you two. I've come to collect you. Chap at the nursery says we'd get a better meal at The George and Dragon pub and there's a play area for the kids. Oh heck! Sorry.' He goes downstairs laughing. 'I recommend a few more clothes before we leave.'

'We'll be with you in a minute,' Jane says.

'Okay, I'll wait in the car.'

Thea and Maddy finish their lunch and agitate to go out and play. Barry and Granddad Warburton oblige with supervision duty. The women stay inside and order coffee.

'Mrs Warburton,' Margaret says, 'Frances and I would like to invite Dee and the girls to come back with us to Hattersley this afternoon. Dee has probably told you that we've plenty of room and lots of space in the grounds for the girls to play. I'm sure that you and Mr Warburton could do with a rest after three months with a toddler on the premises...and so much anxiety. Jane will be an extra helping hand. She's on holiday for the next fortnight.'

Dee looks across at Jane who avoids her eyes. She's studying the ceiling as though she has nothing to do with the suggestion. Dee looks at Frances who nods, encouraging her to accept the invitation.

'Thank you Margaret,' her Mum says. 'It's very kind of you. Dee and the girls will enjoy a change, if you're sure it's not too much trouble.'

Jane, Frances and Dee's mum go outside to tell the girls they're going for a holiday. Margaret catches hold of Dee's hand and detains her.

'That okay with you Dee?' Margaret examines her face. 'I've been watching you and Jane over lunch. You both look as though the sun has come out from behind a cloud. Does it mean that you've arrived at the very best of all conclusions?'

'It means that Jane and I have acknowledged that we love each other.'

'That in my estimation is the very best of conclusions. And will you be happy to have Frances and me as mothers-in-law as t'were?'

Dee laughs though, in the light of a recent remand sentence, there is a sobering side to this question.

'Margaret,' she says gaily, 'if my pleasure in your company continues as it began, I shall be a very fortunate daughter-in-law, as t'were.'


Thea and Maddy are delighted to hear that they're going for a holiday to the big house where Mummy stayed with Margaret and Frances. It doesn't take long before cases are packed and it's time for farewells.

'Thanks for everything Mum and Dad,' Dee says and they hug. 'I hope you have a good rest after your troublesome daughter and her offspring depart. See you soon.'

Barry sets off before them with Thea and Maddy for passengers. Frances drives the Daimler with Margaret in the front passenger seat. Jane and Dee travel in the back, sitting close to each other and holding hands.

# HOLIDAY AT
# HATTERSLEY HOUSE

The arrival at Hattersley is taken up with the girls checking out Julia's flat and bouncing on the beds. Dee puts their clothes away in the empty drawers.

The rest of the afternoon is spent exploring the many paths in the grounds, trailing fingers in the pond, hiding in the shrubbery and collecting windfalls in the orchard. Margaret and Frances relax in reclining chairs on the patio. Jane and Dee stroll after the girls.

'It's agony to be so near you and not able to touch you,' Dee confides while Thea and Maddy hang over the edge of the pond, counting gold-fish.

'Wait.' Jane smiles knowingly.

Dee doesn't have to wait long because the children disappear along the shrubbery path. Jane pulls her in among the leaves and folds her in her arms. They kiss lovingly.

'Mummy are you hiding? I can't see you.' Maddy calls out – and when she does spy them, 'Mummy, why are you cuddling Jane?'

Dee can't help laughing. 'Because she's very nice to cuddle, don't you think?'

Maddy offers herself up to test the quality of Jane's cuddles and plants one of her smacking kisses on Jane's cheek.

'Yes, now I'm going back to Margaret.'

But Thea is looking serious.

'Shall we sit down? Jane says and they sit on a garden bench with Thea in between them.

'You were kissing Jane, Mummy.'

'Yes, I was.'

'Is that because you love her?'

Dee hugs Thea. Her question makes it so easy. She doesn't say, 'Why are you kissing Jane?' because she's realised the truth of their relationship. 'Yes Thea, I love Jane.'

'And I love your mum,' Jane says. 'Is that all right with you Thea?'

'Yes, I s'pose it's all right. Will you sleep with her like Daddy did with Sarah?'

'Yes,' Jane answers for her. Dee's gut thrills at the prospect.

'Will I have to keep out of the bedroom like I did at Sarah's house?'

'Not if you come knocking at a sensible hour. After half past seven I suggest, now that you can tell the time.'

'What if I'm ill?'

'I'll sleep with you.'

'That's all right then. Does that mean that we can stay here for longer than a holiday?'

Dee laughs again. 'Thea, you are a little madam! Would it suit you to stay here?'

'I like my own house...but it's nice here. I'm going to find Frances.'


Left alone, Jane rests her arm along the back of the seat where her hand can caress Dee's back and shoulders or draw her close for more kisses.

'You will come and live here won't you Dee? The house and its inmates can adjust to two children and one more adult. If Mum's wishes are anything to go by, you'll be welcomed.'

'Your mum suggested that we stay here for a fortnight. Consider my destitute state. I have to go home to get a change of clothes unless you're going to let me raid your wardrobe.'

'I'll sort out some clothes for you but I'd like to take you shopping tomorrow. No, don't protest, allow me the pleasure.'

'I will have to go home Jane. At the moment, being here feels like unfinished business. The three of us need to return to our possessions before we can consider uprooting ourselves. Don't you think we're jumping the gun to talk about living together? We hardly know each other. Tracy Manners would say it's of primary importance that we test whether we're sexually compatible for a start – and have you thought that you'll be sharing me with two children? Can you cope with the fact that they'll have to be considered at every turn? I've a divorce to arrange and a home to sell though Jon will probably deal with that…and what about money? There'll be maintenance for the girls but I'll have to work.'

'Slow down a bit! As for the last concern, could you think of me as the partner who earns the money for both of us?'

'Oh cripes no, that hadn't crossed my mind! It seems perfectly acceptable for a husband to keep a wife and children, but I hadn't thought about you keeping me. I'm not sure that my independent streak will be comfortable with being a "kept" woman.'

'Dee, I'm a rich woman. My salary is more than enough to keep two people, I have savings and I own a third of Hattersley. I wouldn't be much help around the place because I'm not very practical. Organizing our home life would be your job. Wouldn't it be part of sharing a working relationship?'

'Say we don't work out, I would feel I ought to pay you back.'

'Do you feel you have to pay your husband back?'

'Actually no, I don't.'

'There you are then. Of all the problems that could beset us, I never thought money would be an issue,' Jane says seriously. 'I'm afraid it's impossible for me to imagine myself in your shoes.'

'It helps that you realise it is an issue,' Dee says.

'There you are then. Tomorrow we go shopping.'

Dee knew she was likely to come up against this sweeping control if she shared her life with this powerful woman, a woman moulded in the Pennyfields' pattern. It was exciting to be carried along by concern for her needs but she must take care not to become too compliant, as she had in her marriage.

'While we're raising difficulties, have you thought about my work,' Jane says, 'and the fact that it takes me away from Hattersley for the inside of every week, sometimes at the weekends. When I'm on duty I live at my flat in town. I often have to attend civic functions.'

'The practicalities diminish the rosy glow don't they?'

'Dee, if we can't air our concerns, and talk our way through problems and practicalities, we might as well give up any hope of a permanent relationship now, before we upset the girls and Mum and Frances. I want us to last. I'll soon be forty! I've been out with nice polite men who were scared of me, I've had the fling with Monica and that's all. I want to live happily ever after with someone I love. I did hope I would meet someone as great as my dad. You'd have liked my dad, Dee. He would have enjoyed your sense of humour. He used to take me abroad with him on some of his business trips. Japan was the last country we visited together. It was cherry blossom time. Dad held up a petal that he picked off my shoulder and said, "No human being can make anything as wonderful as the fabric of a petal Jane." Come to think of it, I remember a prisoner wanting to talk about petals to divert my attention from her impertinence.'

'The prisoner can't see that she was out of order in that instance as her impertinence had the desired effect.' They smile at the memory of that awkward moment. 'Was it on that trip that Julia's silk kimono was bought?'

She nods. 'Anyway, I didn't meet anyone like my dad. What did I do instead? I met a feisty woman called Dee who cares about people, a lovely, courageous woman who demolished my post-Monica self preservation with one outburst of flattery. She made me feel I could trust her. Well, it wasn't just the flattery...' They need a few minutes to hold each other close.

'There are some wonderful aspects to consider if you do decide to come and live here Dee. Have you realised that Mum has no grandchildren? Julia, Barry and me, we've all been disappointing in the procreation stakes. Mum has said that she and Frances would really enjoy having children around. Oh yes, it's all been well discussed. I can see Thea being attached to Frances. Their quiet ways will suit each other whereas Maddy will get on with Mum. You'll be here in the daytime to look after Maddy when Thea's at school. Mum and Frances will be free to fulfil their usual activities and they'll baby-sit when you and I want to go out. You might come into town once a week and we can do a show or see a film. Look on the bright side Dee, the practicalities don't dim the rosy glow. We will of course have to attend to the Tracy Manners evaluation before we finalize the arrangements.' She smiles wickedly.

At bedtime Margaret wants to bath the girls. Frances goes for a walk in the grounds. Jane and Dee wash the dishes and tidy up in the kitchen – where the only gadgets Margaret permits are a fridge and a washing machine – most food is kept in the large cool pantry.

'You take all the time you need to settle the girls down,' Jane says.

'It will probably take a long time for them to get off to sleep and you do realise that we might be wakened early by two excited children?' Dee says anxiously.

'Stop worrying Dee! Think "forever" and "now" will fit into place. There'll be plenty of time for us. The day will come when we'll wish the girls were still small enough to want to come into bed with us. We used to wait till Dad got up and then run in to Mum for a few minutes before it was time to get ready for school. I had to make room for Barry and Julia once they arrived.'

'We did exactly the same.'

'You see! Learn to relax and let things happen. I'll be waiting for you, only a few yards away along a corridor. I'll leave the door open.'

Dee's heart is full as she sits in the armchair in Julia's bedroom. Jane cares. She's Margaret's daughter, strong and powerful and beautiful. Dee has always maintained that "good" can come from every situation. The quality of this "good" is beyond anything she could have imagined. She was so raw and hurt before her arrest. The fight at the prison was an explosion of her repressed feelings. She sulked with Elspeth and was looked after patiently until she was well.

'Are you still there Mummy?' Thea is finding it difficult to sleep. There have been too many changes in her life recently.

'I'm still here. I'm looking out of the window at the little fountain. I can see some thirsty birds having a drink before they settle in their nests for the night. I can see a nice path, over beyond the garden wall. I think that tomorrow we'll go exploring.'

She hears romantic music coming from Jane's flat. Louis Armstrong's grating voice croons, '*We have all the time in the world.*' She breathes out and notices that she's been holding her shoulders high and tense. She must learn to be less anxious. Her lover is teaching her a thing or two about herself – and she's waiting for her. She treads across the soft carpet, kisses the sleeping Maddy and Thea, and goes out into the corridor leaving the bedroom door slightly open. Now, it's her turn.

She closes the door of Jane's flat and Jane opens her arms. She feels indescribable joy, almost reverence as she's held close to this woman. They move as one until the end of that record, and a second and a third, as though they can't bear to be physically apart. They kiss, gentle sensitive kisses that unlock tightness and flood with passion.

'I want you,' Jane whispers into her hair and leads her through to the bedroom. 'Shower I think.'

Slowly and deliberately they undress each other. There's no sense of hurry, of chasing through preliminary exploration to arrive at genital satisfaction. This is the rapt caress that Dee has hoped for; someone who loves the curves of her limbs, the softness of her flesh, and excites her whole body until it's alive with feeling. From Jane's openness to her touch she discerns that Jane is as keen to welcome her kisses, her fondling and stroking. Her sensuous self has found a partner with whom she can communicate her desire but the mutual adoration stimulates them to a heightened degree of wanting.

'Now...shower,' Jane murmurs urgently.

Once in the shower Jane is the lover and Dee succumbs to the soapy warmth and wetness, to the lips that drive her crazy, to the jet of water that undoes her control and reduces her to a long anticipatory moan of pleasure, until she's compelled to release her orgasm in response to her lover's fingers.

They towel each other dry, smooth on fragrant body lotion and, wearing their silk kimonos, lie on the bed.

'I would venture to say that there's a satisfactory degree of sexual compatibility in our relationship,' Jane offers.

'Too early to say,' Dee replies. 'That was a very one sided sortie into sex. You certainly have the wherewithal for me, now there's something I want to try.' She unties Jane's dressing gown belt and exposes the beautiful body. She takes her time to cherish with kisses Jane's neck and shoulders, arms, breasts abdomen until she arrives at her pubic hair. She slides her arms under

Jane's thighs, thrilling at the feeling of possession, of holding her lover trapped in her arms. Her hands are free to reach up and hold her lover captive while her tongue rouses the sensitive places that make Jane gasp and contract, gasp and contract, until she feels the shudder and hears the sigh of her satiated partner.

'Might be a satisfactory degree of compatibility,' she says, drawing the kimono to and tying the belt. She snuggles up against the woman she loves and they fall asleep in each other's arms.

# DECISIONS

On Sunday evening two weeks later, Jane drives the holiday makers from Hattersley to their home. Thea and Maddy are impatient to renew acquaintance with their toys and shoot off upstairs to the bedroom.

'Everywhere looks very tidy,' Dee says appreciatively. 'It was nice of Sarah to make me feel welcome in my own home and lay a fire. It looks as though Jon has got himself another practical partner.'

Jane looks through the kitchen window. 'They've tackled the grass too. It was getting long when I saw it.'

'You've been here?'

'Yes well...as I was beguiled by a certain prisoner called Dee Livesey, I thought I'd better ring her husband and have a talk with him. I wanted to check her story. Thea was at school of course.'

'That was a good idea. So, you've been able to imagine me at home all this time.'

'I've been able to imagine you here very clearly and it's made me uneasy. Your home is attractive, thanks to your home-making talents, and it's going to be hard for you to part with it. I'm worried in case your children and your life here are more precious to you than the possibility of a new life with me. I'm half afraid to leave you but I'm going to tear myself away. You need to be alone with your children and your surroundings and make contact with your friends, but being away from you will be hell. When can I see you?'

'Come for tea on Friday and stay over?'

'I'll look forward to that. Meanwhile, let's not phone. A week of no contact might help us to evaluate the situation.'

Jane calls upstairs to let Thea and Maddy know that she's going. She and Dee say their fond farewells before leaving by the back door so that Dee can inspect her car. She tries the engine and it turns over satisfactorily.

'Someone must have kept an eye on it,' she says delightedly, 'now I can get about. I don't think my lovely new clothes match my pink banger do you?'

'You look like a well to do woman who has an eccentric mode of transport.'

They walk down the drive together and Dee, too shy to hug goodbye in case a neighbour sees them, watches sadly as Jane's Jaguar pulls smoothly away. She experiences a moment of pure fear as the car disappears from sight. She's been loved and supported for weeks and now she's on her own. She unpacks Margaret's bag of overnight provisions. The three of them can shop locally tomorrow. She must do something to keep herself occupied, look round the garden? No, she needs the company of her children. She joins them upstairs until their bedtime.

The evening is cool. She puts a match to the fire and makes herself comfortable on the sofa. She's not surprised to hear the patter of bare feet and see Thea come into the room. They sit cozily under a rug and watch the flames.

'This is nice Mummy, just you and me. I missed you so much ...there's always other people around.' She sighs.

'Shall we make a rule that wherever we go, we grab a few minutes like this each day?'

'Where will we go Mummy?'

'As far as I can see, there are two choices for us. Do you know old Mrs Vine's house, next door to the shop? It's been empty since she died. I could buy that. It has two bedrooms, one for you and Maddy and one for me. The bathroom would be downstairs. I can go to college and re-train to be a teacher. I could afford for Mrs Cairns to help us one day a week. We'd need somebody to meet you and Maddy when you come out of school and somebody to look after you if you were ill. It would be just us. I think we'd manage fine.'

'What about Jane?'

'I have to think what's best for us darling.'

'Does Jane want us to live at Hattersley, me and Maddy as much as you?'

'Yes, she knows that we have to be happy about being together.'

'That's nice. I like Jane. But Hattersley doesn't feel like our house does it Mummy?'

'You're right, it doesn't at the moment, but Margaret, Frances, Jane and I discussed all sorts of ideas about how we could combine Julia's flat and Jane's flat and make a home for the four of us – if we did go to live there.'

'How could you do that?'

'We wouldn't need two kitchens for a start. You and Maddy would have the two big rooms in Julia's flat for your bedrooms, each with comfy furniture so you can invite your friends in. You'll each need a desk, and Jane suggested a television and music centre. Wouldn't you be spoilt brats? The bathroom is fine for the two of you. Julia's kitchen would be changed into a study for me. Jane has her own study and we would share her lounge. The kitchen in Jane's flat will be our kitchen and I'll make the meals.'

'So it would be like our home wouldn't it? I think I like that idea better than Mrs Vine's house.'

'But how do you feel about sharing me with Jane?'

'She makes you happy doesn't she Mummy? I watch your face and it lights up all shiny when you look at her.'

Dee hugs her perceptive little daughter.

'But I don't know any other children who have two mummies. Won't they think it's funny?'

'Yes, they probably will. What matters is whether you and Maddy are okay with two mummies. You'll have three grannies, don't forget.'

'And we'll see Daddy?'

'Yes, I'll ring him and we'll talk about visits.'

Thea yawns.

'You pop upstairs to the loo and jump into bed. Put your bedside light on and I'll show you what Elspeth used to give me.' Dee carries up hot milk and toast and honey and sits on the bed until Thea is asleep.

Her own double bed feels large and empty. The separation from Jane hits with a pain that makes her gasp. She scrambles out of bed and rummages in a drawer for a nighty. If she covers her nakedness with a garment she might not miss being close to Jane's fragrant warmth. It's barely an improvement and she flattens her body, face down, to ease the ache. She couldn't make herself live without Jane.

In the morning, Thea and Maddy are happy to play in the sandpit while Dee mows the grass and begins the weeding of the flowerbeds. They take the pushchair down to the shops and call in on Charlotte and her five year old son Stephen. Charlotte is delighted to see Dee and the girls disappear into Stephen's playroom with juice and biscuits. The two friends sit in the sunny lounge and drink coffee.

'You look wonderful! Is that what a spell in prison does for you?'

Dee pulls a face and lifts her hair so that Charlotte can see the scar.

'Ah...not very nice! Where've you been? We were all expecting you back a day or two after the Hearing.'

Dee tells the whole story. She watches closely to see how Charlotte reacts to the information about Tracy Manners. She doesn't exhibit shock so she proceeds to the news about her love for Jane.

'That can't make life easier for you,' Charlotte says gently. 'My favourite aunt's a lesbian and she has to play her home situation down because of prejudice. But if you say you might go and live in this superb house you won't exactly be under the nose of Mr. and Mrs Joe Bloggs will you? Can we come and visit?'

Dee throws her arms round her friend – more tears.

'Silly ass, did you think I'd cast you off? Do you want me to tell the other mums?' Dee nods. 'We can't be sure of their reactions, can you cope?'

Dee shrugs her shoulders. How can she answer at this stage? She probably won't see much of the mums in future.

'When will you go?'

'If Jon agrees to put the house on the market we can go immediately. We have to settle Jon's access to the girls. I've got to tell him, and Mum and Dad, about Jane and me. I'm not sure they'll be as understanding as you. Dad won't be happy. I'll go over to Burylane on Wednesday.'

In the evening Dee rings Jon. They talk about the details of her return and the sale of the house. He will put the house on the market. 'Do you want to see the girls on a regular night each week Jon?'

'Sarah and I thought Friday night would be good, end of the school and working week. We'll fetch them, and bring them back on a Saturday afternoon – longer holidays we can arrange later.'

Dee is particularly pleased that she'll be without the girls for Jane's visit, this coming Friday.

'I see you've got yourself another chauffeur,' she ventures.

'It's a better car though.'

'That wouldn't be hard. Jon...the prison governor...'

'Miss Pennygorgeousfields?'

'You noticed.'

'How could I not! She's a stunner. Is she really a Miss?'

'Yes, she's a permanent Miss or Ms.'

'What a waste.'

'Her partner doesn't think so.'

'He's a lucky bloke.'

'It's not a bloke.'

'Christ! She's a lesbian!'

Dee ignores the exclamation. 'Her mother, Margaret Pennyfields, has invited the girls and me to move to Hattersley House as there's plenty of room and I can be of practical help in the house and grounds. We'll have to come to some arrangement about transport for your access days when that happens. By the way, it's Miss Pennyfields' home as well as her mother's. She and I will be living together.'

There's a silence at the other end of the phone.

'Dee are you sure you know what you're doing?'

'I'm sure.' She doesn't want to discuss it. 'I'll see you on Friday about four.'

Dee's mum and dad are pleased to see them. The girls make a beeline for the shed and their store of toys. Dee talks about Hattersley and the lovely holiday they've had.

'Nice top and slacks Dee,' Mum says.

'Jane took me shopping so that I didn't have to wear her clothes.'

'Dee if you need money Dad and I will lend you some. I never thought to ask. I assumed Jon would see you all right.'

'Mum and Dad, I'm going to live with Jane Pennyfields at her home. She will provide for me and Jon will give me maintenance for the girls.'

'How do you mean, live with her?' her dad asks tetchily.

'I'm in love with her and we'll live together as a man and woman do.'

'It must be that family! I never thought you would be a lesbian!' Dad explodes. 'What will we tell people?

As Dee expected, his first thought is for what the neighbours and their friends will think. 'What will you say to people Dad?'

'I don't know... There's not just your mum and me that have to cope with this, Dee; there's Agnes and Robert and their families. They're not going to like it I can tell you.

He looks angry and flummoxed.

Her mum steps in. 'We can say that you've gone to share a house with a woman friend,' she says firmly.

'Aye, that'll do, that's the ticket,' her dad says with relief. 'Now I think of it, it's none of their business anyway. It's your life. I just hope she makes you happy Dee. You've had a devil of a time with that husband of yours.'

'You tell us when you're settled in and we'll come and visit,' her Mum says.


Dee gets a shock when they arrive home. She stops the car behind a Land Rover that has been parked in the drive. She and the girls walk round it in amazement and peer through the windows.

'It looks brand new Mummy,' Thea says.

'It does indeed. Let's see if there's any explanation in the house.' Maddy runs to get there first.

'Mummy, there's a letter and two keys.'

They both watch wide eyed, Maddy hopping from one foot to the other, as Dee opens the fat envelope and draws out a certificate of ownership, an insurance document and a note.

'You need a car to match your clothes,' she reads. 'You like odd vehicles and this one is serviceable as well. Enjoy.'

Of course Jane could arrange the documents! Where better to have all her personal details than in a filing cabinet in a prison governor's office?

'What does it say Mummy?'

'It says that Jane has bought us the car for a present.'

'Ohhhhh!'


At four o'clock on Friday afternoon, Thea and Maddy hurl themselves at their father when he appears at the back door. They go off happily with their rucksacks packed with pyjamas and a change of clothes for the following day. Sarah considerately waits in the car. Dee can meet her at a future date. Now there's a two hour wait for Jane's arrival.

Dee lays the table attractively and prepares the smoked salmon starter. She's decided to reproduce the meal she was not able to enjoy at the hotel, the night before her Hearing. The main dish goes into the Rayburn slow oven and the vegetables are ready in the steamer. She hasn't made *Gefulte Orangen* for years and places the creamy sweet in the fridge to keep cool.

The selection of wine used to be Jon's area of expertise, when they entertained. She felt at a loss in the shop, in front of rows of wine bottles. The shopkeeper understood. He recommended Harvey's Bristol Cream sherry and a bottle each of Italian white and red wine.

She's excited. She plays pop music and imagines dancing with Jane. If she sees Jane's hips move to music she'll be undone. A woman once said to her, "what do you feel when you look at him?" – Jon that was. She was embarrassed at her lame answer. "I melt when I see my partner," the woman said, "my loins melt." Now Dee knows what the woman was talking about.

She's nervous too. How has Jane found their week away from each other? Is she still keen for them to live together? Was there any special significance in the new car?

Her careful planning means that she has time to bath, wash her hair and revel in her newly acquired fragrances. She dresses with care; ties her shirt in a knot so that her waist is bare, and unfastens enough buttons to reveal her cleavage. She's enjoying her figure as never before.

She's overjoyed when the Jaguar pulls into the drive and drinks in the sight of her handsome lover. Seconds later, knowing that she has safely turned the key in the lock, she praises net curtains and privacy. Passion throws the two of them onto the sofa. She's only too ready to let Jane overpower her, take off her clothes and claim her breasts. She wants her to cradle her head and tantalize her with kisses that drive her wild. And then her want is concentrated on the lovely woman kneeling astride her. She bares the beautiful breasts and buries her face in their softness, her hands smooth and stroke, circle the wide open erogenous zone until their matching breaths shorten and they reach a feverish pitch of desire. They give to each other and take from each other, mingling their cries of satisfied love.

The two of them rest, in naked contentment, Dee thinking how wonderful it is to be able to trust and give herself completely; to have Jane trust and want her. The fulfilment of the passionate embrace is a new experience. She lifts her head to look at her lover, hardly able to believe this joy and that it could be forever.

'I hope you feel like eating?' she says when they stir.

'I do feel like eating, I'm starving. I've been looking forward to eating alone with you privately, much nicer than in a restaurant.'

They disentangle themselves and start pulling on clothes.

'Dee, tell me first, what have you decided?'

'Yes...Thea, Maddy and I would very much like to make our home with you at Hattersley. The girls enthused about the alterations to the flats that we suggested and Thea in particular insists that you and I need to be together.' She's surprised to see Jane's eyes fill with tears.

'I didn't know how to carry on with my life if your answer was no.'

'You needn't have worried,' Dee comforts her. 'Do you remember when you made me mad and I flung at you, 'and I was prepared to adore you for the rest of my born days?'

'I remember very well.'

'It was only because I knew damn well that I *was* going to adore you for the rest of my life.'

*My Life Outside* is the title of Elizabeth Lister's second novel, soon to be published. A new heroine, but a familiar character, finds that life after a prison sentence is not without its complications.